LOADZ

~ James Franks ~

LOADZ

James was awakened by the noise of a slamming truck door. As he sat up, he noticed he had missed several calls, four from Toya and one from Chi-Chi. Toya was his absolutely gorgeous wife and the mother of his kids. Two years earlier, Chi-Chi was his direct pipe-line to the Aztec Cartel.

TRUCKER J.

I've been driving the same route for the past six months, which so happens to have a layover in Kentucky. One day when returning to my truck after taking a shower, I was approached by a short Mexican named Chi-Chi also known as Taco. I was a little thrown off by his approach to me. Being a trucker and all, red flags went off immediately. Once I realized he posed no threat, I became more lax. Chi-Chi asked me how long I had been a truck driver, trying to feel me up. I responded by saying the past six years, then got straight to the point – "what's up though?" Now I've heard plenty of stories about how the cartels approached truckers and attempted to manipulate or flat out threaten drivers to transport drugs across the border into the states. Chi-Chi made sure he had my undivided attention as he spoke, asking me how much I made a year, trying to speak English as best he could. "We've been watching you for the past six months" My mind switched into overdrive as I began to process what was taking place. Before I had a chance to respond, Chi-Chi indicated I could make my yearly salary roughly every ninety days. From the expression on my face, Chi-Chi had a gut feeling that he had chosen the right trucker for the task at hand. Again, Chi-Chi never gave me a chance to reply. He handed me a cellphone, told me he would be in touch, then walked away.

TOYA.

Toya had been calling James for the past two hours with no luck. She was already upset that her twins, Jamar and Jason, had spilled juice on her all white throw rug she had purchased not even a week ago. On top of that, James has been on the road for six weeks, so sexually frustrated was an understatement. She needed some dick, so while the twins were taking a nap, she decided to get one off. She checked on the boys before heading to the master bedroom. She closed the door, grabbed the laptop and typed in "two Latinos tag team huge black dick." She removed her jogging pants, lay on her back and positioned herself so she could watch the porn as she played with her pussy. It was so wet that a puddle began to form beneath her ass cheeks as she used her thumb and middle finger to caress her clitoris. She then stuck three fingers in her pussy and began fucking her hand as if she was fucking her husband. While watching one female being fucked from the back while sucking the other female's pussy, she couldn't hold it any longer. She squirted all over her hand and the bed. One nut never did the trick, so she continued until she felt that second orgasm. She let out a high pitched moan as her juices came flowing down. She laid there panting and breathing heavily, her legs still shaking, pussy still throbbing and jumping. She glanced at the phone - still no return call from her husband , she drifted off to sleep.

CHI-CHI.

Chi-Chi returned to the farm to give Hector an update. The compound was about seventy acres. Smack dead in the middle sat a huge ranch style house where several armed guards off to the left sat. Two hanger style barns were filled to capacity with some of the purest heroin and cocaine that continually flooded the states. As he exited his vehicle, he was greeted by one of the gunmen. "Hector is inside. He's been expecting you." Chi-Chi entered and headed to the foyer where Hector was patiently waiting. He looked up as Chi-Chi entered.

"How's it going my good friend? So, how did the American truck driver check out? he asked. "Everything is in place and we are clear for takeoff," Chi-Chi said in a joking manner. "That's what I wanted to hear, but before we give him a load, let's first do a few test runs." "Not a problem boss," Chi-Chi replied.   Hector retorted , "I will contact him in a couple of days, and oh, I hope this one is not like the last one because he cost me millions. I'm afraid that if that happens again, I will not be so lenient - *comprendez?*"

Chapter 2

TRUCKER J.

Still not quite sure what just took place, I climbed into my truck, staring at the phone in my hand trying to figure out why the Cartels chose me out of all these damn truckers. I noticed I had nine missed calls and five voicemails from my wife, Toya on my IPhone 10. I grabbed my phone and called my wife. She picked up on the fourth ring, sounding like I had awakened her out of her sleep. "Hey Sweetie, I see you called a few times. I was taking a shower and the phone was in the truck. Sorry about that." I said apologetically. She answered, "Um hum, anyway when are you coming home? Me and the boys are missing you. Shit, this pussy is missing you." I assured her, "I should be back tonight. I have a load to drop here in Kentucky then I'm headed back to the City. Tell daddy how bad that pussy misses me. I know you've been playing with it without me," I teased. Toya burst out laughing. "Yeah, but it ain't like the real thing. I need you," she said. "I know, I need you too, Mrs. L.B." That's a nickname I gave her. It stands for *loose booty.* I love the way that ass jiggles when she walks. "Well, hurry up so I can put this loose booty all on that dick!" I laughed, "you crazy bae." She chuckled, "yeah crazy for you! Love you. See you tonight." "Love you too," I said before ending the call.

RICO

Meanwhile, Rico is shooting his one – two, just leaving one of his little duck off spots. He steps onto the porch dressed like the typical drug dealer, rocking a billionaire boy's club jogging outfit with a fresh pair of Foamposites, and the way he rocked his dreads! He adopted the nickname Mad Max, and it fit him like a glove. With a short temper plus always something to prove anytime a body pops up, you could guarantee Rico had something to do with it. He runs with a group of wild boys that call themselves "The Fam." His right-hand man is a high yellow young'un named Gino, but the streets call him Gunner. Now they are not kingpin status, but they have the Fleet area on smash, and don't nothing move unless they say so. Rico was headed to his all-white Q-seven when he noticed a red S-Five Fifty coming down the street. He thought to himself *this hoe ass west side nigga.* West Side Bill was from 85th and Detroit but had a few drops in the Fleet area. As he rode pass Rico, they locked eyes for a brief second. See, West Side Bill does not bar none. He wasn't worried about Rico or his squad, but truth be told, the only reason Rico hadn't taken a look at him was because his old head told him Bill was off limits. That would soon change. Rico jumped in his whip and called his right hand man Gino. As soon as Gunner picked up, Rico began talking aggressively. "It's about time we show that nigga from the Westside how we really get down." Gino asked "Who you talking about, that nigga Bill? I thought you said your old head said dude was off limits." "He did," Rico answered, "but all we gotta do is make it look like somebody else did it. Meet me at the spot."

TRUCKER J.

I have been home the past couple of days enjoying my down time with Toya and the boys. I was gone for six weeks, so all my time is devoted to them. We've been to Dave and Busters, Sky Zone and today, I think they have plans for us to go to Kalahari. Toya is in the bathroom bathing the twins while I'm in the living room stretched out across the sofa watching my favorite TV show, Animal Planet. A phone rang, and I noticed it wasn't my iPhone. I called out to my bae "somebody is calling your phone sweetie." She yells back "my phone is sitting right here on the bathroom sink, it must be yours." Instantly, I jumped up to retrieve the phone from the master bedroom. It was still in my pants pocket, which I had tossed in the dirty clothes bin. "Hello?" From the other end, I heard Chi-Chi. "Hello my friend; you will receive your assignment in forty-eight hours. The details will be sent to your phone. Once the package is delivered, I will be in contact." "Hold up a second," I interrupted.

"What about my payment?" "Everything will be sent to your phone, just be ready," he said before hanging up.

I put the phone on the dresser just as Toya and the twins walked into the bedroom. "Daddy, hurry up and get dressed. We are waiting on you." I headed to the bathroom to take a quick shower. As I stood under the water, I thought to myself, *what have I gotten myself into?* Whatever lay ahead, I have two days to get myself mentally ready. Toya stuck her head in the bathroom, "Bae, can you please hurry up? Your boys are driving me crazy!" I hurried and got dressed, grabbed my keys, and made sure the alarm was set before we walked out the door. Once in the car, I asked my wife if she made sure she grabbed everything we needed since we planned on staying all weekend. Kalahari here we come!

Chapter 3

CHI-CHI.

Chi-Chi was at the farm making sure the load was ready for the test run that would be in a couple of days. There was the pickup location then the drop off location, but they also had to make sure this new driver they were dealing with was trustworthy. Who is to say he wouldn't just drive off into the sunset with the load, which would be suicide, but you never know, with millions of dollars' worth of product. Not only was there a tracking device attached to the trailer, but there was also a prearranged traffic stop that would take place somewhere along the route to see how this new driver would hold up under pressure. If he failed this test, he would be executed immediately. Chi-Chi couldn't afford any fuck ups. The last driver he picked turned out to be a total fuck up, and to top it off, it later came out that he was giving information to the Feds, which cost the Cartels millions in product and cash.

After making sure everything was good to go, Chi-Chi left the farm and headed to Hector's humongous mansion that sat in the hills of Jurez, Mexico. As he pulled up to the estate, it looked more like a small army base with so many armed gunmen standing around. Chi-Chi exited his vehicle and disappeared inside.

TOYA.

Toya had on a two-piece bathing suit that did her no justice. Standing at five foot two and weighing 148, you would never guess she had kids, let alone twins. As she was getting out of the pool, that ass was all over the place. She was turning heads left and right and I got a little jealous. While the twins and I were still in the pool, I noticed she picked up my phone as if she was answering it, spoke for a brief second then put it back down and waved me over. As I approached, she had a look on her face as if something was wrong. "What's up,?" I asked. "Rico just called," she interrupted. He said you need to call him asap - it's important." With Rico, you never know what to expect.

I didn't want to ruin our weekend, so I told her I would call him Sunday on our way back. I gave her a kiss and headed back to the pool with the boys. As I was walking away, she yelled out "what's your name sexy?" I turned around and said, "you gotta ask my wife that." We both burst out laughing. We've been together sixteen years, but we keep it spiced up so we fall in love with each other every day.

RICO.

Rico and Gino aka Gunner were at the spot they had on Fifty Fifth and Fleet. As usual, the traffic was non-stop. You would have thought they were giving away free food, but everyone knew this was a well-known dope spot. Gunner was in the kitchen serving each junkie one by one as they came through the back door. Rico was in the living room just ending a phone call. He called his old head, but his wife Toya answered. She told him she would relay the message. He was walking towards the kitchen looking down at his phone in his hand, wondering why his old head hadn't hit him back yet. "Ay, yo Rico, Gunner said they said this shit a ten plus. We fuck around and take the few drops that nigga West Side Bill got. Shiddd, we're gonna take them anyway. That nigga on borrowed time. He just doesn't know it! Hurry up and take care of them. We gotta shoot out to Maple so I can drop this money off to my Uncle Moby, and make sure you put that grinder and compressor in the garage. Don't leave that shit in the house." "Nigga, if you so worried about me leaving this shit in the house, why don't you go put it in the garage?"

Gunner lay back in the passenger seat twisting one up as they rode through Garfield. Rico dialed his uncle's number to let him know he would be there soon. As they pulled up, Moby was standing in the driveway putting charcoal inside the grill. "Let me get this grill lit," he said; "then we can go inside and chop it up. That shit smells good. Let me hit that." Gunner passed him the blunt and told him to be careful. Now this ain't that shit you be smoking." Moby laughed, hit the blunt a few times and instantly started coughing. Rico and Gunner looked at each other and burst out laughing. "Told you!"

Sunday Evening

TRUCKER J.

Toya, the boys and I were headed home from Kalahari. I figured I would give Rico a call to see what was going on. He answered on the first ring, so it had to be something serious. "What's up youngin – what's going on?" he asked. "Shiddd, I need to bump into you like yesterday. Something I need to holla at you about in person." "But where are you at right now? He asked. "I'm at my Uncle Moby house." "Cool," he said, "I'm on the freeway. Blow down at the crib in an hour and make sure you are by yourself." "Alright, let me shoot Gunner back down the way then I'm going to fall through." As I hung up, I glanced over at my wife. She was knocked out. I couldn't help but smile. I love everything about this woman even the way she snores!

RICO.

Rico dropped Gunner off on Fleet so he could finish downing the rest of the

Package while shooting back to Maple for a sit down with his old head (he always says two heads are better than one). Before Gunner got out the whip, Rico said, " I know my Uncle Moby's shit is fire, but he is taxing us! I want to see if I can get my old head to turn us on to one of his old suppliers. Shit gonna be fire,and we're gonna get it for a cheaper price." "Do you think he will do it," Gunner asked; "Shiddd, it's only one way to find out. I will call you and let you know the verdict." As soon as Gunner exited the whip, Rico pulled off busting a right onto Fleet, making a left towards Newburgh on Washington, a left onto Harvard then a quick right on to I-77 towards 480. He was on the freeway for ten minutes, and got off at the Warrenville exit.

Chapter 4

TRUCKER J.

I was in the kitchen pouring myself a drink. My wife looked tired, so I volunteered to get the boys situated. She smiled and said, "I love you." I said to her, "I know - I love you too." After I tucked the boys in, I made my way to the bathroom to wash my wife's back while she was in the shower. It's the smallest things that makes a woman feel appreciated, and I had no problem letting my Mrs. L.B know she was my everything. A car pulled into my driveway with music a tad bit too loud for my liking. I opened the side door shaking my head as Rico got out of his Q-seven saying "my fault." I locked the door and called out to my wife, "I'm about to holla at Rico for a minute, then I will be up. I won't be too long." "Okay," she answered, "make sure you set the alarm before you go to bed."

As soon as Rico and I reached the basement, he got straight to the point. "I need you to turn me on to one of your old connections. My Uncle Moby is tearing my mouth out with those high-pass prices, I'm copping five to a thousand grams at a time, and this is every other week." "Okay look," I assured him, "when I get back I will set something up. But the first time you do some hot shit, it's over you hear me? "Yeah, I hear you." "You better, cause this shit ain't no game. You can't push reset when you fuck up. That's your ass, feel me? Let me walk you out, and turn that fucking music down when you come over here! I will hit you up as soon as I get back' – bet!"

GUNNER.

Gunner's phones were jumping. When Kevin Gates made that one song, 'Two phones,' he was talking about Gunner. This last package was gunsmoke. Rico and Gunner smacked the fuck out of it and it still can take a one and a half. They're still saying it's a strong ten. Gunner was sitting in K's driveway in a rental on 57th and Fleet. Unlike Rico, he never drove any of his personal cars to the Hood. He's a young wild head, but he's a thinker. He treats life like a game of chess -- every move counts. His baby momma and his daughter are his queens and He is willing to protect them by any means necessary. As Gunner was pulling out K's driveway, a red S 550 blocked his path. Now Gunner is known for busting shit and his F and N was on his lap locked and loaded. West Side Bill jumped out with his cell phone to his ear. He ended the call just as he reached Gunner's driver's window. Gunner let the window down and couldn't believe this nigga had the nerve to walk up on his car. "What's up?" he asked. West Side Bill said "I'm trying to fuck with you. Everybody going crazy for this shit you and your man is putting out here." Gunner looked Bill straight in his eyes as he spoke, "you know my nigga Mad Max don't fuck with you, so what makes you think I'm gonna fuck with you?" Bill reached into his Louis Vuitton man bag and pulled out thirty thousand, but before he could speak Gunner said, "nigga I make money, money don't make me. Now if you will, I got somewhere to be; this money is calling." Just then, both of his phones began ringing. Bill walked back to his car, got in and drove off.

Next Day

TRUCKER J.

A text came through about 6:00 a.m. I was just getting out of the shower and I already knew who the text was from. I grabbed the phone off the dresser and read the text. It was the details for the load I was scheduled to pick up, transport and drop off in that order. I would be lying if I said I wasn't nervous, but it's too late to turn back now, and after the conversation I had with Rico last night, this direct pipeline might just be more lucrative than I thought. I got dressed, ate breakfast with Toya and the boys and grabbed my over the road bag. As I was walking out the door, Toya yelled "Bae, you're forgetting your head set. Once I was situated in my truck, I put the address Chi-Chi sent me into my truck GPS. I was a little relieved that I was picking up the load from a city called Belen that is actually located in New Mexico instead of Mexico itself.

Three and a half days later, I pulled up to a warehouse that sat amongst a few other building structures. I backed the trailer into dock number three like I was instructed. I was also instructed not to exit the cab. I assumed they were done loading the cargo because a

Mexican came out of dock number two, walked up to my truck and gave me three envelopes. Adjusting a semi-automatic weapon that hung from a shoulder strap, he nodded his head, as the signal was good *to go*. I drove for the next few days until I reached Louisville, Kentucky which was located right next to Cincinnati, Ohio. As I was exiting the highway, a weird looking police car flashed its lights. I pulled to the shoulder of the road after displaying my turn signal. I quickly got my license and paperwork out and rolled down the window. The officer approached with a grin on his face "license and paperwork please," he said. I handed him my credentials and asked why I was pulled over, thinking to myself I was doing the speed limit and my seat belt was in full display. "Oh, just a routine traffic stop buddy. You wouldn't happen to have anything illegal aboard your cab or trailer now would you?" he asked. "No sir!" "Ok, let me go run this and I'll be right back." He returned handing me my license and paperwork and said "have a good day sir." Man, that was close! My GPS showed I was fifteen minutes from the drop off point. The address was located on a dead-end street where two abandoned looking warehouses sat.

I pulled my truck behind the one my GPS directed me to. Dock number six bay was open, so I backed my trailer into it. Like before, I was instructed not to exit my cab.

After they unloaded the cargo, I was given the signal to go, nervous, chest pains and relieved all at the same time. I wasted no time getting back on the highway and headed home.

Chapter 5

CHI-CHI.

Chi-Chi was at Hector's estate discussing business as usual. When his phone started ringing, he answered "hello Amigo, how is it going my friend?" "Well I'm calling to let you know the load has been delivered and the American passed the test," I reported. "That's good to hear. Time for phase two. A large shipment will be headed your way in a week or so," he said as he disconnected the call. Chi-Chi turned to his boss, Hector, and began informing him about the American driver. Hector was very pleased. He instructed Chi-

Chi to get the next load ready. "It's time to put our new friend to work." They both smiled and raised their glasses in a cheer.

Chi-Chi left Hector and headed to the farm. While en route he called James. He picked up on the second ring " Hello", he answered. "Hello my good friend. You did very good. How did you like your three envelopes?" "I can't complain," he answered. "You can't complain? You're talking as if you're not satisfied with it my friend." James retorted, "I'm definitely satisfied. I've never made a hundred and fifty thousand in a week before. But I do need to have an important discussion with you." "These phones are safe to talk," Hector assured him. "Speak your mind.", "Ok, well, "James began, "I have this buddy who deals in heroin and I was wondering if you can supply me and I can supply him and others. It's in high demand in my city and it's like a gold mine. I've ripped a little in my past, but never on this level, but I know if you lay something on me, I can get rid of it." "Tell you what I'll do," Hector replied, "you have a load in a week or so to deliver; after you make the drop and once they remove the cargo from your trailer, there will be four crates left behind. That will be your package - two hundred kilos of pure you will be responsible for. You will owe me two million - that's ten thousand per kilo. Do you think you can handle that?" James crunched the numbers in his head then responded, "not a problem." "Okay, I will send the details to your phone. Be ready my friend," Chi-Chi said before hanging up. As Chi-Chi pulled up to the farm he yelled to some of the workers "meet me in the barn, we have a lot of work to do."

TRUCKER J.

It's been two days since the run from Mexico and my little phone meeting I had with Chi-Chi after securing a direct pipeline. I had to hit the streets and start making contact with the right individuals. I called all my ex-partners and set up a meeting so I would have everything ready to roll. I'm playing on a whole-nother level. There is no room for error. I hit Rico and told him to meet me at Scorchers on Miles so we could shoot a few games of pool, smash some wings while I put my plan in motion. There were a few patrons in the sports bar. I placed our order and got some change and headed to the pool table closest to the bar. For the next two hours we ate, drank, shot pool and chopped it. Rico couldn't believe I pulled a rabbit out my hat. I found better products at a way cheaper price. Of course, I couldn't tell him I was being fronted by the Cartel so I made up some bullshit story; but I had everything in place. Now it's time to flood the city!

RICO.

As Rico was pulling out of Scorchers, he couldn't help but be hyped. His old head just layed some news on him that was about to change his life. Not only did he just find himself a hook, but they were going to front Rico ten kilos out the gate on his old head's name. He'd never seen that much dope in his life other than in a movie; but he didn't have a doubt in his mind that he couldn't move it. This is every dope boy's fantasy. He was about to flood the streets, and either you were going to spend your money with him or you were going to spend it on your funeral. Cleveland streets were about to witness something they had never witnessed before. He popped in an old school CD by Nas and turned it up. His system was screaming "They can hate me now, but I won't stop now" as he pufFed on his blunt, thinking to himself *the streets are mine*.

Next Day

GUNNER.

Gunner had been calling Rico since the night before with no luck. Finally, Rico hit him back. "What's good?" "Shiddd you tell me." Rico replied. "How did it go with your old head?"

"Shidd we in there like swimwear. We bout to flood the streets my Nigga." "You're talking like he plugged us with the Cartel or something," Gunner retorted. "You might as well say he did, and our new connect bout to hit us with ten whole ones." "Stop playing Nigga!" Gunner interrupted. "Does it sound like I'm playing? It's a go.We gotta step our shit all the way up." "Yeah you right, get the squad together it's time we put a little money on the floor, What were you thinking? Just get everybody and meet me at the spot. "Bet"

TOYA.

Toya woke up and looked over and noticed James dick was semi hard. He was still asleep. She positioned herself in a reverse cowgirl position and eased down on it. It slid right in because it was already wet. She began to grind in a circular motion. She felt a pair of hands spreading her ass cheeks and she felt James thrust upward into her pussy with so much force a deep moan escaped her mouth. She looked back and commanded, "give mama that dick!" and he gave her every inch. He flipped her onto her back and put his face in her pot of honey, sticking his tongue in her pussy while he stuck his finger in her ass. She went crazy as he lifted her legs putting his dick back inside her and fucked her fast and hard until she came all over his manhood. He released and pushed it deep up in her pussy. They kissed and held each other until they heard the twins. She looked at James and announced, "you're off today, so they are all yours!" With a smile on her face, she stuck her finger in her pussy then stuck it in her mouth. "Hurry up and get them situated - I'm ready for round two!"

Chapter 6

WEST SIDE BILL.

West Side Bill was still not feeling how Gunner played him the week before when he approached him about some street dealings. Bill was about six years older than Gunner, so he assumed Gunner would have had no problem doing business with him on the strength. He knew Rico didn't rock with him from the stare down and the vibes he got when they bumped into each other at the same clubs. That is why he tried to cut into Gunner. Bill had the West Side on lock for the past five years, but this shit Rico and Gunner have been putting in the streets had him losing clientele left and right. If he didn't figure something out fast, he most certainly would lose the hold he has on the west side.

What he has learned over the years is that there is no loyalty in the dope game; the only thing that an individual is loyal to is the drug or the money. One thing he knew for sure was the streets had no heart; they give you everything you desire then take it all back. But WestSide Bill had a trick up his sleeve. The connect he had just couldn't match the quality of the H that Rico and Gunner were getting their hands on. His only option was to put a play down. He was pulling onto Case off of 45th to holla at some young wild goons who he knew were perfect for this demo, and would put down a helluva demonstration. He parked in the second lot, got out and was greeted by three young boys who looked no older than sixteen or seventeen, but don't let their baby faces fool you, they are known to get busy. He chopped it up with the youngsters for twenty minutes before shooting back to the West.

HECTOR.

Hector's jet touched down on a private runway somewhere in Tijuana, Mexico. He was just ending a call with one of his buyers back in the States, an individual who runs one of the biggest organizations in Miami. He walked off his jet and got in the back of an all black truck. Chi-Chi closed the door and walked around and climbed in. As they drove towards a very important meeting with a few high ranking members of the Aztec Cartel, Hector asked Chi-Chi if he took care of the rearrangements for the next load. "Yes boss, everything is in place," he answered. "I just have to send the American the details." "Good," Hector said. "But we have a huge problem back in the states. Our Miami friends have relocated to Vegas, so you must find someone to continue to move our product." "After the meeting, I'll get right on it." Chi-Chi answered. As they approached their destination Chi-Chi asked what was the purpose of this meeting. Hector answered, "we are having problems with Lamia Cartel, so we're scheduled to have a sit down with Diablo and his under link this is the only way to avoid an all out turf war. Wars are bad for business. Now come on so we can get this over with so I can get back to my estate. I have two of the sexiest ladies I ever laid eyes on."

Two weeks later

TRUCKER J.

I received a text message from Chi-Chi with the details for my next run and, of course, my package will be aboard with the load. Like usual, I packed my bags for an over the road trip. Since it was still early in the evening, I decided to take Toya out for dinner. The boys were at their grandmother's house. I will hit the road first thing in the morning. We were just finishing up our dessert when the boys started blowing up our phones non-stop. I guess that is what happens when you teach five-year olds how to use the phone. We picked them up and headed home. Toya was tucking the twins in and I was in the basement on the phone making last minute contact with everybody just to touch base. I need everyone in position and ready to roll at the drop of a dime.

When I got upstairs, Toya was already in bed with her phone in her hand playing candy crush. I gave her a kiss and jumped in the shower. I climbed into bed and was out like a light as soon as my head hit the pillow. I was awakened at three thirty a.m. when my alarm went off. I got myself together and headed out the door.

Thirty minutes later, I was on the road. This time, I was instructed to pick up from a location in Santa Fe, New Mexico. I made the pickup and headed to the same warehouse in Louisville, Kentucky. I made the delivery and now I'm on my way back to the city, but I'm not out of the woods yet. I still have two hundred kilos of pure H that I have to get back to the city. Nine hours later, I was safely pulling my truck into the Southgate Plaza. I park my truck here when I'm not on the road. I walked over to my cargo van, jumped in and pulled it up to the back of my trailer. I got out, opened the rear doors on my van and on the trailer, climbed in and grabbed the dolly to remove the four crates. I loaded them into the back of my van, locked my cab and trailer up, closed the van rear doors, hopped in and pulled off. No one will ever guess I was driving down Libby Road in Maple Heights, Ohio with two hundred kilos of pure H in a van 'man.' I was headed to the Life Storage Facility. I rented a storage unit there two weeks earlier. There is no way I could put two hundred kilos in my home and feel safe. I pulled up to the Life Storage, punched my code into the key-pad, pulled through the gate, up the hill and to my storage unit. I unloaded three crates and left one in the van. I locked the unit, jumped back in the van and headed to the crib.

As I pulled in my driveway, my motion light came on. I pulled my cargo van into the garage, closed the garage door and set the alarm I had installed on the garage two weeks ago. As I said, I have no room for error. I used my key to enter the side door, dropping my over the road bag in the hallway, I disarmed and reset the alarm. I was so tired, I didn't have the energy to take a shower. I stripped down to my boxers and climbed into the bed, snuggled up to my wife and fell asleep.

Chapter 7

WEST SIDE BILL.

For the past three weeks WestSide Bill had his three young boys laying on Rico and Gunner. It's just a matter of time before they put the play down. Bill was at the carwash on 116th and Corlett. The only reason he was up that way was because he was meeting this nigga named Young Work from 113th and Benham. His hook was OT at the time, so he sent him to his dude who had up the way in a headlock. Young Work pulled up in a cocaine white 2018 AMG Benz truck. He jumped out rocking black Robin's jeans with the shirt to match with red stones all over his back pockets that matched his all red, red bottoms, Bill hopped out wearing Gucci everything with a mean ass Bust Down on his wrist. They dapped and walked off to the side, choppin it up for a few minutes. Bill followed Young Work over to his AMG. Work reached into the backseat and grabbed a bookbag and handed it to Bill. Bill walked over to his S550, dropped the bag on his passenger's seat and opened his glove box. He grabbed two large stacks of money and walked back over to Work, handing it to him and said "twenty-five bands on the head. It's all there, "bet."

They dapped again, going their separate ways. Bill rode down Union and blew his horn as he drove past a group of young boys at the corner of 103rd and Union. They were standing around their cars - a 460 Lexus, a black Jag truck and a candy green Harley on a 26 inch rim, The cars belong to some up and coming young hustlers from that hood and the owner of the Harley was his old head Trucker J, their O.G, who I didn't see out there, so he must have been inside the store.

TRUCKER J.

 I woke up late as fuck! It was going on 10 a.m.   I didn't hear the boys, and neither did I smell breakfast in the air. I guess she took the twins to daycare and didn't wake me because she knows how tired I am when I come home from a long run/haul. I jumped up, took a real quick shower, got dressed and headed out back to the garage. I stufFed twenty keys into an army duffle bag, then locked the van, closed and set the alarm on the garage and jumped in my car. As I was backing out of the driveway I called Toya. "Hey Baby, I see you finally up." "Yeah, I got a lot of ripping and running to do today," she said. "I will see you when i get back. Love you." "Love you too," she said.

The second call was made to Rico. He picked up on the third ring. "What's good?" "You. Meet me at the spot on Cullen. It's time to get rich," I said laughing. "Say no more. I'm on my way," he said. I got to the spot, took ten keys out of the duffle bag and put them in a Sav-a-Lot bag, I had to use two Sav-a-Lot bags. I went into the house through the back door. When Rico got there, I was setting the keys on the table. His eyes lit up and damn near jumped out of his head, he said sounding like a little kid, "so this is really happening?" I responded, "today is Xmas. Ho-Ho-Ho! But on a serious note, ten kilos at $70,000 a kilo is $700,000. Before you say anything, this is 100 pure. You can turn one to two, or three. It's up to you how you do you, but I'm gonna need $700,000 in 45 days. Is that gonna be a problem? He was stuck. This is what you wanted. The City is yours for the taking. Why be a prince when you can be the King? 45 days Rico."

RICO.

Rico put the two Sav-a-Lot bags in the truck of his rental. He knew he couldn't drive his q7 to his old head's duck off spot. He jumped in his rental and pulled off headed to his stash house located in the old Brooklyn area on the

Westside he called Gunner and told him to put the word out they got it and for the low and to meet him at the stash house, only him and Gunner know where this spot is located not even his old head knew. As Rico pulled into the driveway, the four Rottweiler's came running to the gate on high alert. These dogs were his babies. He opened the gate and pulled the rental up to the garage, closing the gate back before grabbing the Sav-a-Lot bags. He went to the back door and grabbed one of the many big bags of Diamonds dog food and filled up the four dogs pans and their water buckets. He entered the spot and set the Sav-a-Lot bags on the floor in the empty kitchen. The only things in the house were a dining room table and chairs. All the things they needed sat in the corner - a huge grinder, a huge press, gloves, two face masks, a box of narcotize (but the hood slang is *Narcan*, and a pint-sized bucket filled with Quinine, a drug that is used to cut heroin. You can never be too safe, especially when dealing in a dangerous drug. He was placing the grinder and press on the table when Gunner walked through the door. He told him to bring the bags that were on the kitchen floor. He snatched them up and headed to the dining room. "Damn! We are about to do all these today?" he said. "Shit, we might be here all day and night. The sooner we get started, the sooner we will be done," Rico said. "They put on gloves and the face masks and began removing the keys from the bags. Stacking them on the table, they busted one open and put it into the grinder. "Where is the scale and the scooper?" Rico asked. "Oh, it's under the kitchen sink. I'll grab it," said Gunner, Gunner walked back into the dining room and placed the scale on the table. He moved the paint bucket full of quinine next to the table, took the lid off and scooped up a pile and dumped it onto the scale. The scale read 498 points, He dumped that into the blender and opened one of the kilo's of H and scooped another large amount, dumped it onto the scale. It read 522 points. He removed 20 grams from the 522, dumped the remaining 502 into the grinder and closed it. Pushing the button, it began grinding and blending the H. with the Quinine. This is how they turn one into two. They call it *putting one on it.* They repeated the process over and over. As each key was turned into two, they compressed them back individually and put eighteen in their stash spot inside the floor.

Just as they were finishing up, Gunner and Rico's phones began to ring. Word was out they had it for the L.O. Rumor was they busted a move. O.T. niggas could care less what they did. All they knew is they had fire and they wanted parts. Niggas were coming from everywhere to cop. They pulled up to their trap spot on 55th and Fleet. That bitch was jumping so hard they dumped two keys in 4-1/2 hours and still had about eight more plays.

Rico grabbed the duffle gym bag with the money they just made and walked out the side door. In his left hand was a 40 Cal with an Extendo. He popped the trunk and put the duffle bag inside and closed it. Just as he was getting in the driver's seat, three young dudes ran up the driveway with black ski masks covering their faces. This type of shit Rico aka Mad Max lived for. He didn't hesitate. He stuck his left hand out the window and let that forty talk - *BOC BOC BOC BOC BOC!* The three masked men fled, returning fire in process, Gunner heard gunshots and got low. Grabbing the Drako from the corner, He came out the front door ready to let a nigga have it. He was still in a crouch position. As the last dude was running out the driveway, he was shooting up the driveway. Gunner thought he could be shooting at only one person – Rico. Gunner raised the Drako, and before the mask man could clear the driveway, he was lifted off his feet by the impact of the rounds spitting from the Drako. He was dead before he hit the ground. Gunner continued finger fucking the Drako trying to hit the other two niggas running up the street. Rico called out to Gunner "we gotta get the fuck outta here. All that shooting, I know somebody called the police." "Alright, I gotta grab the phones!" Always being a thinker, he turned off all the lights and locked the door. He ran and jumped in the passenger seat still holding the Draco. Tires squealing as Rico smashed off.

WEST SIDE BILL

West Side Bill sat chilling at the Broiler on 64th and Detroit waiting for the waiter to bring his bag of food out to him. He was in deep conversation with Mad, the owner, until his phone started ringing. When he viewed the number, he knew it was his young boys from Case. He answered, "tell me something good." The person on the other end spoke as if he was crying. "They killed Duke! Shit fucked up." "Who killed Duke? Bill asked. "Them niggas on Fleet you sent us at. We were laying and watching how they move. We followed them to the West Side, but we lost them so we went back to Fleet and waited. When they pulled up, they had that bitch lined up like it was a block party.

We waited about 4-1/2 hours. Later, the nigga with dreads came out the side door with a duffle bag and about the time we ran up on him, he already put it in the truck and was getting in the car. I guess he saw us, cause before we got all the way up on him, he stuck his hand out the car door and started busting. We took off and Duke started shooting back. The other nigga came out the front door with a chopper letting that bitch go. Duke got hit. That was my right hand, and I won't rest until them niggas dead." "Alright, look," Bill encouraged him, "let me figure something out.

I'm going to hit you back later, and let Duke's people know I will pay for his burial."

Chapter 8

GUNNER.

Man, who the fuck was them niggas? Gunner asked. "How the fuck I'm supposed to know? They had on masks nigga!" Rico snapped. "You know you gotta get rid of this car." "Naw! For real?" "We can't go back to that house any more. That bitch on fire fosho. Now pull up to my car so we can drop this rental off at the dealer." Rico pulled up to Gunner's car, popped the trunk and told Gunner to grab the duffel bag with the money. "It's in your truck, and stay right behind me until we get to the rental spot." Gunner trailed Rico from 71st and Harvard to Lee Road between the top of Kinsman and the top of Bartlett.

Rico jumped in with Gunner and they headed towards Bedford to one of Gunner's hideaways – a nice two-bedroom apartment called Bear Creek. Gunner pulled into a parking spot and popped the trunk. Rico grabbed the bag and they went through two sets of doors. Of course, you had to have a key. They got in the elevator, rode to the fifth floor and walked down the hall to the left. They got to apartment 503, acting as if what they had just been involved in was nothing. Rico dropped the bag in the living room and walked into the kitchen, grabbing a bottle of Remy. Pouring himself a drink, he asked Gunner where his money counter machine was. Gunner returned from his bedroom with the money counter. inside one hand he had his phone and was talking to his baby's mother. He was telling her he loved and missed her. Rico grabbed the counter out of his hand and started laughing. He said, "you just count this money." Gunner said "shidd, that's what the machine is for!" He sat on the couch and started flicking through the channels.

TRUCKER J.

After Rico left with the 10 keys, I was thinking, he believes one of my buddies is fronting him on the strength of me. He has no clue I am the person supplying him the product. I still had ten more units to move before I headed back home. I called my old head, "Old Blue." He was pushing sixty, but he still had a mean hustle hand on him and he ran through bricks like a 21-year old runs through hoes. He told me to stop by. It took me 20 minutes to pull up to his house on 118th and Buckeye. I left three units higher and I knew Blue would have the money before the 45 days were up. I called my young hitter who lived on Benham.   He had a squad that did numbers. If he ever got a Cartel plug, I feel for the City. I blew down and dropped him five units. I laid five on him and he wanted to cash five out. I told him I would get with him in the morning.

One more stop to make – to my dude White boy Lenny, also known as Project Lenny. He thinks he is black and is more crazy than a muthafucka! He got the Lorain area on lock, but he also has a lot of out of towners and they spend real money. I pulled up to his spot on 73rd and Colgate. Never again. So much traffic back and forth I started not to stop, but Lenny's crazy ass was outside and he saw me, so I couldn't keep going. I let him get in and I pulled off, bent a corner and dropped him off in the alley behind the spot. This nigga so crazy. He said "wait I'm gonna give you the money now." I looked at him like you got over $140,000 in the trap spot - you big tripping." He started laughing and said "$140? You mean $1.3," and got out and went through the back door of his spot. He came back out in less than five minutes with a footlocker bag and handed it to me through the window and said "next time bring me five," and walked back towards the house.

TOYA.

Toya was wondering where her husband James was. He had been gone all day and hadn't called. It was getting late. She put his plate in the microwave, washed the dishes and was about to take a shower when she heard the side door motion sensor. "Bae, is that you?" she yelled. "Who else is it gonna be?" James replied. "What did you cook?" he asked. "It's in the microwave," Toya answered and asked, "Why haven't you called all day?

You could have at least let me know you were ok." "Damn, my fault. I got a little rushed and I had a lot going on." "You had so much going on that you couldn't call your wife and check on your kids?" she snapped. "You must have come on your period today, cause you are tripping," I retorted. "A wife being concerned about her husband is tripping?" she said. "Okay," I said, "I apologize I didn't call you. Are you happy now?" "No," she answered. "No, and I'm going to bed and please don't touch me. Goodnight! Toya stomped off to the bedroom and laid in bed hot and bothered. That's why she's upset. She hasn't had none all day and she refused to play with herself when her husband is not away at work. So, as soon he steps foot in the bedroom he's gonna give it to her and she's gonna take it. Either way, she's getting some head and fucked in that order - plain and simple!

TRUCKER J.

Wow! Wifey on a rampage and I know why. All she gotta say is "I'm horny," but no, she likes to fuss and throw tantrums and pout. But I can't lie. That shit turns me on! She knows when I come to bed that I am gonna fuck the shit out of her. My dick hard just thinking about it. After I was done eating, I rinsed my plate and grabbed a bottle of wine off the counter. I then headed to the bedroom. As soon as I opened the door, all I saw was a pussy. Toya was laying on her back, her naked legs wide open. Her inner thighs glistening from her juices. She acted if I wasn't standing there watching. One finger, two fingers, three fingers. Before she could get to four fingers. I moved her hand and stuck my tongue in her ass and fucked her ass with my mouth. I attacked her pussy with rough sucks, fingering her at the same time. She nutted all in my mouth. I didn't stop. I laid on my back and made her straddle my face and ride it until she nutted again. Then I gave her what she was craving. I stood up and lifted her up onto my dick and fucked her standing up. Then I made her get on her knees and stuck it in nice and slow. I did it from the back and was teasing her. I said beg for daddy's dick. She looked back and said "please Daddy, fuck . . . fuck me." I began giving her long deep strokes. I quickened my pace until I was fucking her like I was a mad man. We both came at the same time, breathing heavy and sweaty. We lay there holding each other until we fell asleep.

Chapter 9

RICO.

Fleet was still on fire from the shooting last week, but Rico couldn't take a break. He owed his old head $700,000. He and Gunner had been dumping kilos left and right. They ran through four more within the last week and made $600,000 in a week and one day. If they keep this up, they will be playing with a million in no time. They had to shut down the spot on 55th and Fleet, but they had other spots on 53rd, 57th, and 61st, so it didn't slow anything down. Since that shit happened, Rico and Gunner stay on full alert. They still haven't heard anything; no info on the robbers or who sent them. The only thing they know is it was some down the way niggas, because the young boy who got killed was a known shooter from Case Court,

Rico had just left the stash house in Old Brooklyn and brought out four units. He had a sale for three, but was going to put one in the hood and let the young niggas eat and collect those couple dollars on the back end. See, if you eat and look good and your hood is not eating and looking good, you begin to look like food to them. So, everybody around me gets a slice of the pie and it makes your hood build a wall of defense around you because they protect the source of income. You put work in the hood - they make money, you make money and everybody is happy. I hooked up with my people from Akron. They cashed me out for three and paid me for two more. Them niggas getting some money in Akron. I gotta shoot all the way back West, but if it's cool for $200,000, I would have driven all the way to ATL, and that's a 10-hour drive. Shid, I move money. I had them meet me by West 25th Street by the Zoo on Bridge at the little rinky dink gas station across from Burger King just before you get to

Broadview. They made 1.1, got one unit in the streets and still got eight Kilos's left. Rico called his old head and told him he had that light "seven" for him.

TRUCKER J.

I woke Toya up eating that pussy. Her pussy tasted good and had that sex smell to it. I love how it be all creamy the morning after our fuck sessions, and I go crazy when I see her toes curl. She is trying to act like she still sleeps until I nibble on that clitoris. She loses it and starts cumming everywhere and making these weird sexy grunts, and the faces! Oh my God, that shit is making my dick throb so hard, and when I nut I just stay in the pussy. It feels like I'm in heaven!

Hours Later . . .

As I was getting out of the shower my phone started ringing. I answered and it was Rico. "What's up youngin '?   Come grab this little change I owe you," he said. I said "stop playing. It's only been two in half weeks. You can't be done." "Naw, I ain't done, but I got that. "That's what's up," I said. "Just swing by and drop it off. I'm just getting up." "Yeah right," he replied. "Your old freaky ass has been eating pussy and ass all night. You are an old freaky ass nigga." I replied back, "If you go tell it, tell it right! I've been eating pussy and ass plus slanging nine inches of horse dick all night and all morning; I'm 'bout to blow through with that bread."

After Rico fell through and dropped off that bag, I chilled with the twins while Toya ran a few errands. We played with their toys then ate peanut butter and jelly sandwiches for lunch. I put them in the tub and got them dressed. Toya was still out, meaning she was at the salon getting her nails and hair done. I knew she wasn't coming back any time soon. I put the boys in their safety seats, strapped them in and jumped into the driver's seat of my 2017 Ram truck. I opened the moon roof and blew the horn at my next door neighbor who was cutting his grass as I pulled out of the driveway. I finally made it to Wal-Mart, found a parking spot and got the twins out and headed inside. They both ran to the cart that was fashioned like a car. They both got in, and I headed to the frozen section to grab some shrimp, salmon and broccoli, I heard someone say "Old Head."

 I turned around and West Side Bill, one of my buddy's sons, was walking towards me smiling. We embraced in a manly hug as we greeted one another. "What's going on old man? he asked. "I see you and the boys out shopping. Where is the wife?" "Where else on a Saturday morning do women run off to? I answered. "The salon," we both said at the same time laughing. We talked for a while and agreed to link up the next week. The boys and I made our way to the self-checkout line, scanned, bagged and paid for our items. As I was putting the boys into the truck, my phone started going off. It was my young hitter Young Work from Benham. "What's up? He asked. "You forgot about me this morning. I came to the hood at 9:30 a.m., waiting for your call. It's going on 12:30 p.m." "My fault," I apologized, "my wife dipped on me to go to the salon, so I got the boys. Can I bump into you a little later? "Shidd," he said, "I have no choice. That shit you got is the truth, just let me know so I can make sure I'm in the area…. Bet"

Toya lightweight threw my day off. I still gotta shoot to the West Side for White Boy Lenny and I still got Work waiting. That's $700,000 waiting on me. The only reason I ain't pissed off is because I'm kicking it with my twins, and ain't no amount of money more important than them.

Five Hours Later . . .

It was going on 5:30 p.m. when Toya pulled up. The boys and I had just finished eating and were sitting on the porch blowing bubbles. As soon as she parked and got out of the car, I headed to the garage. Damn, I left my keys in the house. I went back into the house to grab them. I told Toya on my way out that I would be back within an hour, tops. I walked back to the garage and disarmed the alarm, entered and unlocked my cargo van, climbed in the back, removed 10 units and grabbed a bag. I exited the garage, locked it back and reset the alarm. Hopping in my truck, I put the bag on the floor behind the passenger seat and pulled out. I called Young Work and told him I was on route. As I pulled onto East 113th and Benham, I dialed Work's number, but he was standing amongst a group of guys, all wearing black tee-shirts with the word 'MOB' displayed across the front. I admire the unity that his squad\hood displayed. They starved together and got it out the mud and now they balled together. Young Work spotted my truck, walked to the back of a gray impala, grabbed a Gucci duffle bag out of the trunk and walked down the street to where I was parked. He got in and reached over and put the duffle bag on the back seat. I told him to grab the bag from behind his seat then remembered White Boy Lenny's five units. I told him to take five out and put them in the bag with the money he just gave me. He looked at me and said "damn you ain't playing. You must have come up on a Cartel plug." I said "shidd, I wish!" But he hit it dead smack on the nose. We dapped and he jumped out.

I pulled off heading West. I was listening to a new artist out of Dallas Texas, Yella Beezy. He had just dropped the cut called "That's On Me," and it was hard as fuck. As I was getting off the West 44th exit, I called Lenny's crazy ass to let him know I would be pulling up within the next 10 minutes. The sun was just starting to set and the sky was a dark blue/purple color. I turned on to 73rd and Colgate, and just like any other time, it was in full swing. People were everywhere. I parked two houses down and hit Lenny's cellphone. When he answered, I told him where I was parked and to bring a bag out like last time. He came out with a Footlocker bag. As he was walking towards my truck, he stopped a few feet away and began yelling at some dude. He walked up on the guy and smacked the living shit out of him. Dude took off running up the street.

When Lenny climbed into the passenger seat of my truck he was laughing. I asked, "what was that shit about?" He said "an old boy ran off with a zip like two weeks ago." "So, I said, "you out here flipping about $1400, while I'm sitting waiting on you with $350,000 plus five kilos of H on one of the hottest streets on Lorain, not to mention the $350,000 you carry in that dumb ass Footlocker bag. I dug into the duffle bag that lay on the back seat and grabbed the five units from inside. I looked at Lenny and asked "where is the bag?" He said he forgot it. He laid the Footlocker bag on the floor of the passenger seat and grabbed the five kilos. He got out and started walking towards his spot. I watched him, thinking to myself like this dumb ass nigga, he has lost his fucking mind. That's the type of hot shit I don't want no parts of. This will be my last time dealing with dude.

I jumped onto 90 East, merged onto 480 East and got off at the Warrenville exit. A right turn here, another right turn there, then a left turn and I was driving down my street. I pulled into my driveway at 6:45. I grabbed the duffle bag from the back seat and the Footlocker bag from the front floor, got out and walked through my side door that was open. Due to Toya's mom and sister being inside visiting, I headed straight to the basement to put the money up. I had a mean stash spot inside the ceiling. When I was done, I headed upstairs to the living room where everyone was. I spoke to my sister-in-law, kissed my mother-in-law on the cheek, tickled the twins and planted a long, wet kiss on my wife and retreated to the master bedroom to catch *the last of the basketball game. The Cav's were playing Golden State

Chapter 10

CHI-CHI

Chi-Chi was just arriving in Miami. He was sent to the states to seek out someone capable of running the Miami District since the infamous Black Cartel relocated to Vegas. It was Chi-Chi's job to put somebody in position. He had a few candidates in mind, but he had to be 100 percent sure of the individual he chose. As he headed to an upscale night club, his phone rang. It was his boss, Hector. "Hello," he answered. From the other end Hector greeted him. "Hello my friend. Did you ever check on that Miami thing?" "Yes," Chi-Chi replied. "I'm in the states now. It's gonna be a little harder than I thought it would be. Our old friends had Miami on lock, and it's gonna be hard finding somebody to fill their spot and do the numbers they were doing; but I just might know how to fix our little problem. Give me a

few days and I will let you know what I got."
"Okay, call me as soon as you figure
something out," Hector said. Chi-Chi had no
clue how to fix their problem when the call
ended. He was just trying to get off the phone
with his boss because his driver had pulled up
to the upscale night club and Chi-Chi was
ready to party. One of the things he loved
about the states was their nightlife. It is like no
one ever sleeps - 24/7, partying day and night.
Anytime he was sent to the states to
handle business he always found time to hit a
few clubs and fuck a few bad bitches, and once
he gets drunk, he had no problem throwing his
money around. Chi-Chi was in V.I.P with five
sexy females, bottles of the finest Champagne
and a platter filled with a pile of the purest
cocaine known to man. He had already made
plans to take all five women back to his suite
that of course, was a penthouse at the very top
of the hotel, so you know what lay ahead.

WEST SIDE BILL.

West Side Bill felt bad about Duke getting
killed, but it's all part of the game. That is why
he played to win. This morning he was
dressed in an all-black suit with some black
loafers. Of course, they were Gucci. Bill loves
double G's. He was headed to pay his
respects to Duke and his family. He paid for
the service and bought a tombstone, plus put a

couple dollars in Duke moms hand. When he pulled up it was packed. He parked, headed inside and took a seat in the back. It was a nice setup. After the pastor spoke, a few family members said a few words and everyone lined up to view Duke for the last time. His mom went crazy and they had to drag her away. She didn't want to let her baby go. No mother would. After he viewed Duke, he really felt bad. Duke was laying in the casket looking like a kid who was asleep. West Side Bill kind of felt like he was the cause of Duke's death, all because he was ego-tripping and sent Dirty Red, Duke and Dale for Rico and Gunner.

They were putting the casket into the back of the hearse when he was approached by Dirty Red. "What's up?" Bill said. "Shit, just fucked up!" Dirty Red replied. "My nigga gone and Dale couldn't even see his twin laying in the coffin. Don't nobody know where he is. Haven't seen or heard from him in two days. Something ain't right. It just doesn't feel right! He would have called me out of all people. Something ain't right." "Youngin, I feel like this shit my fault," Bill said. "If I would have never put that play together, Duke will still be here." "Fam, you can't blame yourself. We know what we were getting involved in, this shit goes with the game. You win some, you lose some; but I'm about to ride to the graveyard with the family. I will call you so we can chop it. This shit far from over." Dirty Red said.

Three days later . . .

DIRTY RED.

Dirty Red had been riding through the Fleet area, for the past three days in hopes to spot Rico or Gunner. He figured that they switched spots due to the shooting> He still hadn't heard from Dale, and his gut was telling him he was already dead. He thought to himself, "if the streets knew Duke had a twin, I'm sure Rico and Gunner knew too. They probably put two and two together. Shit they would probably know I was the third person if they did their homework. I have to kill them before they kill me!" Just when Dirty Red was about to give up for the day, an all-white q7 rode right past him, and guess who was driving – yep, Rico with Gunner in the passenger seat! Like always, Gunner was telling Rico he thought it was a bad idea for them to be driving around in Rico's personal whip. "We just snatched up that nigga Dale. We gotta move smart until we catch that bitch ass nigga Dirty Red and murk his hoe ass." Rico looked at Gunner and said "fuck Dirty Red! He's gonna get it just like them bitch ass twins got it." Rico pulled up at the light at 65th and Fleet and was about to bust a right on 65th towards Lansing.

Gunner was about to tell Rico to pull off as he was removing the gun from his waist, but it was too late! Dirty Red was already at the driver's window letting that mac off – *TAT- TAT- TAT-TAT –TAT-TAT-TAT-TAT,* glass flying everywhere! Rico hit the gas, but the damage was already done. Seven bullets found its mark; six into Rico and one hit Gunner in the hand. They drove several streets over before Rico passed out. Gunner called the ambulance but not before throwing their guns into the sewer drain. Dirty Red was driving well over the speed limit. He was trying to get away from the crime scene as fast as he could. His blood was pumping. The mac lay across his lap still hot. He couldn't believe he caught them niggas slipping! He knew for sure he murdered them. He let the whole clip off. He felt like his friends could rest in peace now. He was heading to his uncle's house to lay low for a while. He knew this move would have a lot of people upset, but it's too late to worry about that. It's kill or be killed, and he wasn't ready to die!

RICO.

Rico lay in the hospital connected to so many tubes it looked like he was a human experiment. It was touch and go, but he was definitely in bad shape, but he was stable now. There were so many people in the waiting area you would have thought he was the mayor of the city instead of a young street dude. It was total mayhem - women fighting over girlfriend titles, family members fighting over who could talk to the doctors; everyone wants to be in charge and the shit just flat out crazy. Gunner ain't speaking to the cops. There are rules to this shit, but everybody knows Gunner is about to go on a killing spree. He's the type that will snatch your mom on Sunday when she's on her way to church. It ain't a place Dirty Red can hide. The stakes just went up!

Chapter 11.

GUNNER.

Gunner hadn't left his nigga Rico's side since the shooting. He hated seeing him laid up, hooked up to all those damn machines, and to make matters worse, Rico was still in a coma. It's going on day five, and still nothing. Rico's mother entered the hospital room and told Gunner he needed to go home and take a shower and get some rest. Gunner refused. He wasn't leaving until his nigga woke up. Rico's mom saw the hurt and pain in Gunner eyes. She knew it was in vain to ask him to leave his friend's side. She told Gunner she would bring something for him to put on his stomach when she returned. She leaned over and kissed Rico on his cheek with tears in her eyes. Seeing her only son like this was tearing her apart. She gave Gunner a long tight hug and told him she would be back later. Gunner was in deep thought. He couldn't believe he and Rico were that lax, to let Dirty Red get the drop on them. He was more so angry at himself for allowing Rico to drive his personal whip through the hood. Nine times out of ten if they were in a rental, it would have been less likely they would have been spotted.

One thing for sure is Gunner was about to put down a demonstration that would rock the city to its core. He already had some of his youngins following Dirty Red's mother and sister. Soon, Dirty Red will be begging for me to put a bullet in his head instead of his mom, his only sister and her five children. Gunner felt no remorse for children or innocent women. His mother was murdered when he was 11, and he didn't understand how, why or who. She was an innocent woman. That incident made Gunner heartless, and selfish. The only person he really cared for was Rico. They have been friends since third grade, and he was the only person Gunner ever expressed his feelings about his mom being killed. Rico was the only person on this earth that had ever seen Gunner cry tears. He met and fell in love with his baby's mother, and had a daughter later in life. Rico and Gunner's baby's mother and his daughter were the only people Gunner truly cared about. Dirty Red will soon feel his pain very soon.

MARGIELA.

Margelia and his MC's as usual were putting on a mean show. They were pulling up to K.O.D's at least sixty bikes deep, and every bike was custom. Margelia is the co-founder of Lit Life M.C.'s. Yeah they pounded the streets of Miami hard, but he was from Cleveland, Ohio and rumors are he still controlled and ran the Lit Life M.C. 's located in Cleveland. Their clubhouse was located in the 10th Ward. The city says Lit Life is responsible for the heroin that is flooding through the 10th Ward and plenty other areas. As they were parking their bikes, bystanders were pulling out their phones, taking pictures and recording. It looked like a bike show. Any color you could think of was in attendance, and they were patched up representing their colors. See, everybody that was somebody, or getting some money or just visiting Miami knew King of Diamond was one of the places to be on the weekend.

As Margelia and Lit Life entered the Club, they were searched and patted down, then escorted to V.I.P. They had damn near every booth in V.I.P filled, and it didn't take long before every stripper in the building was trying to get to their section. It looked like their section was on fire with all the sparklers attached to every bottle they purchased. They haven't seen a demonstration like this since BMF. They were definitely making a statement that said they ran Miami. They were putting on a helluva movie.

Let the cameras roll, and to put the night over the top, rapper Young Jeezy fell off in the spot and put on. You've got to respect dude - he fell off in that bitch, no security, just him and a few of his partners.

Next Day...

Margelia was laid up in his condo with his son's mother. She lived in Cleveland, but you would swear she lived in Miami. He flew her in every other week. Yeah, he's getting a lot of paper, and females are throwing themselves at him left and right, but he's head over heels for the mother of his son. They finally got up and got dressed, and headed out to go spend some quality time together. Margelia had to make one pit stop at this diner to meet his supplier Julio. They were just pulling up when a short Mexican got out of a limo and entered the diner. Margelia parked and told his lady friend he wouldn't be long.

As he entered, Julio waved him over and began to speak. "I want you to meet someone. This is my boss Chi-Chi." Chi-Chi spoke "how's it going, my good friend?" Margelia stuck his hand out as he greeted Chi-Chi. Chi-Chi was second in command of the Aztec Cartel. He got straight to the point. "Julio speaks highly of you and told me you are the leader of a motorcycle club that has a large portion of Miami in your grips. I summoned you here today because I believe we can help each other. I need someone that can run the whole Miami District. Your only problem will be counting money, because I'm gonna flood you with so many kilos it will take you two months to count them all." Margelia looked at Julio smiling, and Julio said "I told you I had a gift for you. You know this position you're being placed in is a position you can never walk away from." "I'm honored and I definitely will hold up my end, so I guess it's safe to say I'm the new king of Miami." Chi-Chi said "yes it is, my good friend."

CHI-CHI.

Chi-Chi just put someone in charge of the Miami District. Hector would be pleased to hear that, so he decided to give his boss a call and update him. Hector picked up on the second ring, "hello my good friend, tell me something good." Chi-Chi replied, "I found a solution to our problem., I had a meeting with Julio, and he recommended this guy he's been supplying for a while now. He is already popular in Miami, with a well- respected team to back him up. I did a check on him personally and he checked out, so I had a sit-down with him and Julio to discuss the details.

He will deal directly with Julio.   Everything is good to go on this end. When I return, I have to stop by the farm and get a shipment together for a load to Miami. I will contact the American with the details." "Very well my friend, have a safe trip back. I will see you when you return."

Chi-Chi had one more night in the states. He ordered a call girl who was 5'7", thick in all the right places and did tricks with her mouth. He was in his penthouse suite with a pile of pure Coke on a glass table. He was doing a line when she arrived. She stepped off the elevator and straight into the suite. She was wearing a trenchcoat, letting it fall to reveal the beauty that lay beneath. Chi-Chi wasted no time. He guided her towards the jacuzzi. She turned to face him and said "I want to do a line off your dick." He began to fumble with his belt to free himself. She walked over to the table and scooped up a small amount onto the card that was lying next to the pile. She walked back to Chi-Chi, grabbed his manhood and put a line of cocaine along the shaft of his penis. She used one of Chi-Chi's rolled up hundred dollar bills and snorted the line off his dick and placed it in her mouth. She started off with slow soft sucks at first then picked up the pace. She started feeling the effects of the cocaine, and before she knew it, she was bent over and Chi-Chi was going to town. Short, fast pumps and slapping her ass cheeks leaving handprints from the impact. They indulged in so much cocaine they couldn't feel their faces. They fucked like rabbits until the next morning. Once he had enough, he paid her and sent her on her way. He figured he would take a shower and a quick nap before heading to the airport.

Chapter 12.

Back in Cleveland

DIRTY RED.

Dirty Red received a call from his mother. When he answered the phone she sounded as if something was wrong. Red had been hiding out and laying low at his uncle's house in Solon, Ohio. When his mother called his cell phone he had no clue what she was talking about. In a frantic tone, she explained that she noticed that two young boys had been following her for the past three weeks. She notified the police, but since they hadn't actually committed a crime, there was nothing they could do but file a police report. She decided to call her son because she began to worry that something bad was about to take place, and so right she was. Dirty Red told her to calm down, assuming it was just some young punks trying to find someone to rob, and that he would be over as soon as the sun went down. He only went outside in the evening. He told his mother not to go anywhere and to make sure all the doors were locked. To make her feel better, he called his sister Sonya and had her and her kids go keep her company until he got there. His mother said "okay baby, just hurry up and get here as soon as you can." "I will be there mom, stop worrying," he reassured her, "everything is going to be fine." Dirty Red begins pacing the floor back and forth. His gut was telling him to head over there immediately, but his mind told him he couldn't afford to be spotted in the streets, especially once he found out Rico and Gunner weren't dead. He was a wanted man, and they were coming for his head. He had to figure something out, and he had to do it fast.

400 D.NELLE

400 D.Nelle and his right hand had been following Dirty Red's mother for about three weeks now. Gunner put this play in motion because the streets said Dirty Red went into hiding after he tried to kill Rico and Gunner but failed. So, Gunner's plan was to snatch his mother to flush him out of hiding. As 400 and his partner sat three houses down in a White Cargo van, they noticed a car pull into the lady driveway a woman in like five kids get out and go inside, the young boy sitting in the passenger seat looks at 400 and says "what now? She has company." 400 responded saying "shidd, what does that mean? We snatching all of them. Let's go." They got out of the van and walked towards the house.

They didn't want to take a chance to be seen by the neighbors, so they decided to enter from the back.

As they reached the back door, they pulled their masks down over their faces. 400 kicked in the door. In a flash they rushed into the house, guns raised. They were on top of the two ladies and children within seconds. They were screaming loud and shit, so 400 put his gun to one of the kid's head and said "if y'all don't shut the fuck up, I will put his brains all over the wall." He held them at gunpoint while his young partner duct taped their mouths and hands. He didn't duct tape their feet, because they had to be moved to be placed in the cargo van. 400 told his partner to go get the van and pull it up to the back door. Once they had them all secure in the van, they drove off to the location Gunner sent in a text. They didn't care about the family they had just kidnapped. The only thing they were concerned about was the $15,000 that was promised to them.

GUNNER.

Gunner was just pulling out of the hospital parking lot at Metro after visiting Rico. He had come out of the coma, but he still had a lot of healing to do. Just as he turned on West 25th, his phone rang - it was 400. He told him they had snatched Dirty Red's mother, but her daughter and grandkids were with her, so they snatched them all. "That $15,000 we agreed on was for the mom only. That price just went up big homie." "Don't trip. I got you and imma throw a little something on top." I got a few stops to make then I will meet you all at the spot.

Ever since the shooting, Gunner had been so preoccupied with trying to find Dirty Red that he hadn't sold one kilo. He and Rico's phones were ringing non-stop, so he figured it was time to get back to the money. They still had eight units to move. He had his out-of-town people coming from Detroit to grab three, his Nigga Black Dave from 116th and Buckeye wanted two and his niggas Rayvon and Fat Moe from Kinsman wanted three, so he had to shoot to the stash house. As he pulled up, the dogs ran to the gate on high alert. Before going into the house, he grabbed a bag of dog food from the garage and filled their food pans and water bowls. He entered the house through the back door and grabbed the eight kilos from the stash spot in the floor and put them into the two Sav-a-Lot bags laying on the table. He locked the back door and made sure the gate was locked before jumping in his car and pulling off. The Sav-a-Lot bags lay in the back on the floor.

Chapter 13

TRUCKER J.

It had been a few days since I'd visited Rico, so me and the wife decided to stop by Metro and drop in on him. He was doing a lot better, but he still had aways to go. He started laughing as soon as we entered hospital room 303. Only three people were allowed in his room at a time, and the waiting area was packed with individuals waiting to see him. Most were every female he ever f*****.   I looked at him and said "from the looks of things out there in the waiting area, you have your hands full." Winking at me he said "it comes with the game." Toya went off "so what does that statement and him winking mean?" she said to me. She was pissed like it was an Insider joke. She knew nothing, and me and Rico bursting out laughing only fueled the fire.

I chopped it with Rico for about an hour before Toya and I headed to her mom's to pick up the boys. Just as we were pulling in her mom's driveway the phone the Cartel gave me started ringing. I looked at Toya and told her I would be in shortly. She gave me that look and got out and went inside. I answered the call, "How's it going my good friend?"

CHI-CHI.

Chi-Chi was on the phone up in the air in one of their many private jets discussing the details with Trucker J. He informed him about the loads going up to Miami. He asked him how the product was moving on his end. Trucker J reported "it is moving, and I will bring my payment when I pick up the Miami load. I will let you know when I'm all done so I can get another shipment." "Very well, my friend. I will send you the details in a day."

Chi-Chi hung up from Trucker J just as the jet was landing on a private airstrip in Juarez, Mexico. He exited the jet and climbed into the back of an all-black Tahoe and told the driver to head to the farm. Arriving at the farm, he spoke briefly with a gentleman who headed towards the barn to relay the message to start getting their shipments ready for the Miami run. 2000 kilos, 1000 kilos of H, and 1000 kilos of cocaine.

Chi-Chi got back in the truck then headed towards Hector's estate. He arrived and was greeted by one of the many gunmen. Chi-Chi headed to the pool in the back. His boss was sitting at the bar with a glass of champagne in his hand, a few women on both sides of him and one sitting on his lap. When Hector noticed Chi-Chi, he greeted him "how is it going, my good friend?" "Very well. I took care of everything. There will be a shipment to Miami In a few days for our Miami friends. Julio will notify me soon as it arrives." "Very good, my friend. Why don't you join me? It's more than enough to go around," Hector said. Chi-Chi took his jacket off and sat down. Instantly a lady walked over and placed a champagne glass in his and filled it to the top.

DIRTY RED.

Dirty Red called his mother to let her know he was on his way, but she didn't answer. He called his sister Sonya's phone and still had no answer. He began to panic. He ran two red lights, not thinking about being pulled over. The only thing on his mind was getting to his mother's house. As he pulled up, he noticed Sonya's car parked in front of the house. He jumped out without turning his car off. He ran towards the porch, but then thought he should probably enter from the back. If someone was inside waiting, he could sneak up on them. As he approached the back door his heart dropped. The back door has been kicked in. He clutched his Mac 11. There were no signs of a struggle, no blood. He began looking for clues that might tell him who was responsible for this.

Just as he headed for the back door, his phone rang. The screen showed a Private Caller. He answered. The voice on the other end sent chills up his spine and broke his heart. His mother was crying on the other end. A male voice came over the line "your life for theirs, plain and simple or I will start mailing you pieces of their bodies, one by one to your uncle's house in Solon. Oh yeah, I know about that spot. Your sister told me everything I needed to know." Dirty Red realized the person on the other end was Gunner. As Dirty Red spoke his voice began to crack. "Please don't hurt them, just tell me what you want," he pleaded. "I told you already," Gunner retorted, "your life for theirs. Be at the park Broadway on Barksdale. You have until midnight, and if you try to call the police or bring anyone with you, you can kiss your mom and sister goodbye." "Where are the kids?" Dirty Red asked on the verge of crying. Gunner never answered him. He just started laughing and hung up. Dirty Red didn't know what to do. He called West Side Bill. He picked up on the first ring. "What's good, where have you been hiding? He asked. "Them niggers Rico and Gunnar got hit," Dirty Red replied. "I know they found out I was the third person involved in that shooting, so I tried to get them before they got me." West Side Bill said "they said that was you who put that play on?" "Yeah, Dirty Red said,"but it didn't go how we planned, and now they got my mother and sister plus her kids. They said my life for their life." "So what are you going to do?" Bill asked. Dude, they're going to kill you and your family if you give yourself up."So what am I supposed to do, just let them kill my family? Ain't no way! If they going to die for some s*** I did, I feel like I should die too." West Side Bill hung up on Dirty Red while he was still talking.

Chapter 14

WEST SIDE BILL.

Bill couldn't believe his ears. As soon as Gunner gets his hands on the young boy, Dirty Red, he will tell who sent them at Rico and

Gunner in the first place, which will put him in the hot seat. The only two options West Side Bill has is to kill Dirty Red himself or pack up and leave behind everything he has built. He headed to his condo downtown at the Nine. He had over $400,000 put up there. He packed his clothes, shoes and jewelry and placed a call to his son's mother who lived in Detroit. He let her know he was headed that way and to start looking for an upscale spot for him. He needed the address to one of the storage facilities located there. He wasn't leaving his shit.

Bill paid a lot of money piping his condo out, and called a moving company, Two Men and A Truck, to relocate his belongings to a storage unit in Detroit. The only thing he grabbed was the duffel bag with his cash and headed for the door. He left instructions with the front desk for someone to let the movers into his condo when they arrived and for him to be notified. He put his cash in the trunk of his s550 and jumped onto the highway. He still has work that he needed to move, but that was the last thing on his mind. He will worry about that once he is safely situated in his new home. He thought to himself, "shidd, I can hustle anywhere."

Next Day

GUNNER.

As Gunner walked into the house where Dirty Redd and his family were being held, he was greeted by 400. He said "they are in the basement, Big Homie." As they walked through the house toward the basement door, all you heard were the dogs barking in the backyard. When 400 opened the basement door, a smell so foul smacked him in the face and he damn near threw up. I guess it would smell like s*** and piss when you have eight people tied up for two days straight. He went down the stairs and stood before Dirty Red and 400 to remove the tape from his mouth. As soon as the tape was removed Dirty Red started crying. "Okay you can let them go now," he wailed. Gunner responded, "you know how this shit goes. The best witness is a dead witness." Dirty Red began pleading to release his family. Don't do this. I can tell you who sent me at y'all. Please just let my family go. "Start talking and I will think about it," Gunner Said. "First you got to promise to let my family go. They don't have anything to do with this." Dirty Red was begging." "Okay I promise," Gunner said as he winked at 400. Dirty Red began spilling his guts; and the Mastermind behind the reason why my niggaa Rico was lying in a hospital bed is Bill's hoe ass. He must have been in his feelings from that day Gunner shitted on him and his little $30,000. He turned to walk out the basement. Red yelled, "you said you would let them go." Gunner turned back to him and said "God shows mercy, I don't." He looked at 400 and said "you know what to do."

One Week Later…

RICO.

Rico was laying in the hospital bed watching TV when breaking news flashed across the screen. 19 Action News was showing a gruesome crime scene with five children, two women and one man found executed in the basement of a vacant home on Cedar Avenue all shot once in the head execution style. Rico thought whoever did that were cold-hearted muthafuckas. He had been in the streets for a long time, but he'd never involved women or children. Just as the news was going off Gunner walked into the room. They dappe, and Rico said "you see that shit that happened over there on Cedar?" Gunner gave Rico that look, and right then and there Rico knew Gunner was the heartless muthafucka who had the city in an uproar. Before Rico had a chance to ask again, Gunner repeated that look, so he left it alone. He will find out later. He figured this wasn't the place to discuss it. Gunner filled him in on the situation and the fact that West Side Bill was behind the whole thing. Rico couldn't believe it. Hoe ass nigga had the nerve! He knows how we get down, and to top it off a hoe Gunner said she saw some movers taking all of Bill's shit out of his spot four days ago. Rumors were that he left town. He is a smart man, but you know how it goes - when that paper gets low, he's gonna reach out to the old head and we're going to be waiting.

TRUCKER J.

I was en route to the address programmed into my truck's GPS. My destination is Los Lunas, a city located in New Mexico. My pickup point is never the same. This location is not like the others. It was heavily populated with tons of Mexicans. I backed my truck up to the dock. A fat Mexican walked up to the driver's side door and speaking in broken English inquired, "you have something for Chi-Chi?" I reached over to grab that heavy duffle bag that held two million in cash and handed it to him. He took it and walked away. They began to load my trailer taking about 45 minutes to finish. Once they were done, I was giving the signal and I pulled out.

I was headed to Miami to a location in Opa-locka. I pulled up to the factory that was smack dead in the middle of the ghetto. As I pulled my trailer up to the open dock, a black ass man came out of a door that was set off to the side. I recognized he was Haitian by his accent. He asked if the load was for Julio and I said yes. He went back inside and they began to unload the shipment. It took over an hour and a half because they only had one toe motor. Once they were done, I was given the signal and I pulled off.

On my way back, I stopped at a Flying J to refuel and take a quick shower before getting back on the road. When I arrived back in the city it was raining cats and dogs. I parked my truck at its normal spot, Southgate parking lot. I thought to myself, "that was a long-ass ride." I called Toya to come pick me up. We lived less than seven minutes away so she was there in no time. As soon as we pulled into the driveway, the first thing she said was "can I have some of my dick tonight?" Now you know my freaky ass will, of course." We got out and once inside she wasted no time. She was all over me. We made love all night and she was so loud. I was glad the twins were at her mother's for the night. Damn I really missed her touch. I savor every moment. The best part was having her in my arms. When we were done, we just laid there looking into each other's eyes until we drifted off to sleep.

Chapter 15

JULIO.

Julio received a call from Haitian Black that the shipment had arrived. Julio called Chi-Chi to inform him that everything was a go. After talking to Chi-Chi, he called Margelia to arrange to meet him at the factory in Opa-locka. He was in charge of the Aztec Cartel and was known in Miami as the Mexican Hitman, so he had no problems when dealing with the street dealers or gangs. At the snap of a finger, you would vanish. He was headed over to the factory to do an inventory count before he handed the product over to Margelia and Lit Life MCS. He knew with this crew and a little shove there would be no problem moving the product. He and Haitian Black were standing outside talking when Margelia pulled up with a few members from Lit Life in tow.

MARGIELA.

Margelia pulled up in a black Hummer. Behind him was two 24-foot Box Trucks. He got out and walked towards Julio,and some black ass dude who he later found out was Haitian Black. They greeted one another then got down to business. Haitian Black showed the truck drivers where to park while Margelia talked to Julio. "This is your pickup point. Whenever a load comes in, this is where it would be. The only person you deal with is Haitian Black. This will be my only time coming here. When you're done, drop the payment, which is twenty million, off at the diner. Are we clear?" "Loud and clear," said Margelia. They spoke for a few more minutes after which Julio went over and talked to Haitian Black before leaving. After both trucks were loaded, Margelia and Black shook hands and Margelia jumped back in his Hummer and pulled off with the trucks behind him.

They were headed to the Lit Life Clubhouse. It was a building located near South Beach. There was a bar in the front, living headquarters on the second level and the shop was located in the rear and had two huge bay doors. The layout was top-notch upscale. The bar was a wraparound that seated 50 people. It had 15 booths that ran along the outer perimeter. Five televisions hung along the top of the bar and everything was white and olive green in color. The shop had basically every tool known to man. There were two ways to go up to the living headquarters. You could gain access by the spiral staircase in the corner of the shop, or you could take the private elevator next to the main office inside the bar. This elevator required a passcode. The two box trucks backed into the bays. Margelia parked his Hummer and jumped out once he was inside. The two bays automatically closed. He stood back as they unloaded the product. With the Aztec Cartel supplying him, he was about to see the type of paper that could buy a small country.

Margelia's right hand man was a three hundred-pound bald headed light-skinned dude with a short temper. His club name was The Big Man. When he entered the shop, his presence was enough to grab the attention of everyone in the room. He approached

Margiela. "I see the load came in. You're working these n***** like Hebrew slaves unloading all this shit." "If we don't work, we don't eat and you know I like to eat. From the looks of it, you do too!" Margelia said. Both of the men laughed. The product was unloaded and put into a room behind a false wall.

Margelia called a meeting for every Life MC. Every member was to be present at the meeting. He was about to give each individual instructions on what sections they would be controlling. Four hours later the sections were broken up and divided. Some areas were heavily populated with cocaine and crack while others were heavily populated with Heroin. Margelia's new Miami was run by the infamous cartel that was torn apart by the Feds. Rumor has it that they relocated to Vegas and have a few casinos, so Miami had a void that needed to be filled. He and his team were put in a perfect position to take over.

Two weeks later…

TRUCKER J.

I was out and about making drop offs. The only thing good about today was that everybody who was calling was coming full fair, duffle bag in hand. When I say today was a good day, man, Old Blue snatched five units and I fronted five. That's money in the bank. After I left my old head spot, I blew down on Young Work. Like always, 113th and Benham were flooded with foreign cars. Niggas was standing on both sides of the street. A few guys were riding four-wheelers and dirt bikes. Work wasn't playing when he said his team did numbers. Remember, he got 10 his last go-round. This trip, he snatched 15 units, so you know I fronted him 15 units. He said, "you can fool these other n***** but I know you got a cartel plug on this s*** you putting out here and you loaded it." I looked at him and said, "I like you. We're going to have a sit-down real soon. We dapped then parted ways.

White boy Lenny has been calling all day every day, but I made my mind up not to f*** with dude. He do hot dumb s*** , and I refuse to go down for somebody else's mistake. I was headed to Rico's house. It was nice, I just hate the 45-minute drive. He lived out in Stow, but when you're in the game you never want to stay too close to the hood, rule number one - your well-being. I pulled up and was greeted by some big ass dogs when I pulled into the driveway. Rico came walking out from the back. You could tell he was still healing by the way he was walking. I told him to put those damn bears up, cause that's what they looked like. He started laughing and said "you're good." I got out and grabbed a duffel from the trunk that held the 10 bricks. I had to be careful to grab the right bag. I had 1.4 million inside three other duffle bags. I walked into the crib, handed him the bag and told him to get well and take it easy. Since he was still recovering from being shot up, I told him to slow roll. I told him "ain't no pressure." I already paid the cartel the two million for the shipment I was fronted. I told him I would let my people know. It's all good - he was still under the impression that my ex-partner was laying it on him and that's how I wanted to keep it.

I was heading home when Toya called to see what I wanted for dinner. I told her not to worry about cooking. "Call Mr. Wonderful's on Lee and Libby Roads and place an order, I will grab it and be there in thirty minutes," I said. She said "okay, I love you." I could tell she was smiling. "I love you more," I said.

RICO.

Rico just got off the phone. He has been home from the hospital for a month now and is still recovering. Not being able to move around like he wanted to was torture. His old head finally fell through with the pack, so now Gunner could flood the street. They had been out of work for two months since Gunner sold the last eight kilos that were left, but they weren't tripping, They made 1.2 and still had one unit in the street. Rico knew when Gunner pulled up because his dogs started barking. They let Gunner pass because they were raised around him, just like the four Rottweilers at the stash house. Rico let Gunner know to put a two on this batch. After they pay the hook they will walk with a smooth 2.3 off of this flip. "You still ain't found s*** out about West Side Bill yet?" Rico asked Gunner. "Nope, that Nigga got in the wind, but he is a dead man walking. Whenever he pops up he is on the floor (on the floor meaning it's on sight). He grabbed the duffle bag, jumped in his rental and headed to their stash spot. "Now it's time to get this money."

GUNNER.

Gunner was on the freeway headed to their spot in Old Brooklyn. After he Fed the dogs, he went inside and got down to business. Mask and gloves on and grinder on the table, he began the long process of putting a two on the batch. When he's done they will have 30 keys. Letting them go at $100,000 a unit will bring them a smooth three million. He had a long day/night ahead of him, but you know the saying *if you don't work you don't eat,* so he was putting in overtime with a smile on his face. He didn't get done until damn near 3:00 a.m. He most definitely wasn't about to meet anybody at this time of the night/morning. He wasn't even about to drive through Old Brooklyn at this time. Guess the floor it is since they had nothing in the house, he thought. He fell asleep instantly. He was tired as f***. When he opened his eyes, he had to remember he stayed at the stash house.

He had over 30 missed calls on his trap phone and six on his personal phone from his baby's mother. He called his baby's mother first and let her know he was okay. He was so caught up in finishing he forgot to call home and let his lady know the demo. She wasn't worried about him cheating, because they had a healthy relationship. She was more so worried about his well-being. After he ended the call with his baby's mother, he wasted no time letting everybody know it was back on and poppin. He grabbed two duffel bags and put seven units in one and eight in the other. He put the remaining 15 units into the stash spot inside the floor and headed to the trap house on 61st and Fleet. He let everybody know to come to the spot to shop. He wasn't moving around today and he had four of the shooters posted, so if a Nigga played crazy, they might as well get his casket ready. Niggas were coming from across town, down the way and he even had his Detroit people falling through. He dumped six units and it wasn't even two yet. Shidd, the way it was going he might have to shoot back to the stash spot. As he was coming out of the kitchen he flipped. "What the f*** y'all in here playing the game for? Y'all supposed to be on guard, not playing no f****** PlayStation," he said to his young shooter. "That's what's wrong with you young n***** common f****** sense! Protect the bag, and I am the f****** bag!" His phone started ringing. It was Rico. "What's good fam? Gunner asked. "S*** just checking to see how everything is moving," Rico said. "With me pushing the rock it's definitely moving. We're looking real good from where I'm standing." Gunner told Rico he would stop by and that he bumped into Richie Rich and Slim from Detroit.

MARGIELA.

Meanwhile back in Miami, Margiela and his team Lit Life flooded every part of Miami, from the upper class down to the slums. They knew they would have to go to work with a few other crews to prove they were the new Kings of Miami. There was one crew there that was going to be a real problem. They were run by a Latino named Pedro, but the streets called him Looney P. He went to war with the Haitian Cartel, and to prove he was a force to be reckoned with, he managed to kill the leader. It was the way he did it, though. He scalped him from head to toe and drove through Little Haiti with the skin over his body, bloody and all. But Margelia wasn't about to let nobody get in the way of his plan to take over point blank. They have been in several shootouts, and you can bet there will be plenty more. He was on his way to have a sit-down with Julio and get a little advice. He was new to this level of the game, so advice wasn't a bad idea.

TINY.

Tiny was at one of the many spots he was in charge of. Like always, there was non-stop traffic. They had about six armed guys outside - three in a van, which you would never guess, and three in front of the spot. They had to be on high alert. They had hit one of Pedro's most lucrative spots and killed everyone except for one person. They left him alive to send a message. They took no money, instead they set it on fire. Over four million in cash and another three million and product up in smoke. That would let Pedro know Lit Life had hella money too, because they burned every dollar. This will make a n**** madder than robbing him. They figured if they kept hitting all his money spots he would eventually fold, but they didn't know Pedro was no regular person. They had no idea what they were in store for, but it was right around the corner. Tiny had a few guys load today's taking and run it out to the Tahoe. It was close to $800,000. As he approached his white Hummer, just before he jumped in the Tahoe exploded and shook the whole block. Tim was thrown 10 feet from the impact of the explosion and had minor burns, but everyone inside and within five feet of the Tahoe were dead instantly. The gunman came running, but it was pointless. There was no one to shoot at. Someone put a bomb on the Tahoe and used a remote to set it off. They say if you can't stand the heat, get your ass out the kitchen!

Chapter 16

PEDRO.

Pedro got a call from the second-in-charge that the hit against Lit Life went as planned. He said "they are following Margiela as we speak, and he's by himself right now. He's at a little diner. It seems as if he's having a meeting with someone in the rear of the diner." Pedro said "okay, don't lose him. I want to know where their stash is located. The way they are flooding the streets, they must have one of the cartels supplying them, and if we can pinpoint the spot where it is being held, we can hit it and clean them out. Then their supplier will murder them for losing a load that large, so don't let him out your eye site." Pedro returned to snorting lines of cocaine off his sexy woman's ass, then he stuck his tongue in her ass and she began to f*** his face with her ass. She was bent over doing lines off a plate. Her pussy was sloppy wet, and she wanted to be f*****. Pedro stood up and rammed his dick into her ass. She yelled for him to stop, but it was in vain. He f*** her so rough that she began to cry. He was so coked up that he never even noticed. When he was done, she ran off to the bathroom. Laughing, he returned to snorting more coke.

Back in Cleveland.

GUNNER.

Gunner was meeting his people from Detroit. They came through to grab 10, but he only had nine on him, and they were light weight in a hurry, so they just copped the nine and dipped back out; but before they did, Gunner and Richie Rich got to chopping it for a minute, and Richie Rich was telling him how a loud mouth nigga just moved down to the D and was always talking about how he had the west side on lock back in Cleveland, always wearing Gucci. Gunner asked what was dude's name and Richie Rich was like "they call him West Side Bill or some s*** like that." Gunner and Richie Rich dapped and went their separate ways. Gunner called Rico and told him he just found out where WestSide Bill bitch ass was hiding out at, Rico said "yeah, I think it's time for a road trip." Gunner said "hell no! We're getting too much money to put ourselves In harm's way. Let's just put some money on the floor and let the little homies eat. I will send a few of them down there this weekend. Let me holla at Richie Rich and put something together, but I'm headed your way now, and you ain't going to believe how many units we ran through today. Let's just say we are officially millionaires now straight like that!

Back In Miami . . .

MARGIELA.

Margelia was just leaving the diner after meeting with Julio. He received a call about Tiny and the spot being hit. He was furious. The paper was chump change, but his right hand man almost lost his life. He had to put Pedro down, and he had to do it quickly. He did his homework on Pedro and found out he loves bitches. That was his weak spot – pussy. A few years ago, there was a click of chicks who were putting shit down. They were no longer around, but there was a group of chicks out of Cleveland, the Cash Money Chicks, and I was about to fly them down to Miami, and put them on Pedro. *Ain't no way he's turning down some pussy*. Margelia was so deep in thought, he didn't notice he was being followed as he pulled into one of the spots.

Tiny was sitting in the Lazy Boy with burns on his hands, arms and the left side of his body. The look in his eyes said murder. I put him up on me flying the Cash Money Chicks out, and he said that was a great idea. I got on the phone and put the call in, gave them the details, and once we agreed on a price they were headed to the airport. They will be here in a couple hours. Put 24-hour security on every spot, and I want 10 armed guards at the Clubhouse all around the clock. As Margelia was walking to his Hummer, he had a feeling he was being watched, he just didn't know from where.

CASH MONEY CHICKS.

Tiff, Lee and Tee were triplets that called themselves the Cash Money Chicks. They were a group of females that were known for setting n****** up in Cleveland; and where there is robbery there is murder, and when it comes to the triplets, *Redrum* is a part of their game! Tiff was the leader of the three. She was the one who was quick to take charge. It was probably because she was born three minutes before Tee and Lee, soon as the plane landed at Miami International they called Margelia. He sent a car for them and set them up at a hotel on Ocean Drive. He told them he would stop by and holler at them in a couple days. Until then, kick it and enjoy themselves. Everything is on him. He sent a duffle bag with $225,000 and an additional $50,000 for them to do some shopping and sightseeing with until it was time to get Dirty. Once they made it to the room they were in awe. They had been around some Heavy Hitters getting major paper, but they never made this much money and gave extra to shop with.

They wasted no time. They didn't even unpack. They put the duffel bag safely into the room safe, grabbed the $50,000 and headed out the door. The triplets had carmel complexions, stood 5'4", and weighed 140 pounds – no body fat, and they were identical. There was no way you could tell them apart, and the triplets used this to their advantage. They were walking through the mall turning heads left and right with bags galore in their hands. Lee saw some sexy guys standing to the side looking their way. Lee being the nymphomaniac walked right up to the guy who caught her eye and flat out asked what that shit hit for. Her sister Tee said "well damn, at least ask the nigga his name first with your freaky ass." Both groups burst out laughing. The triplets ended up spending the day with the group of guys they just met.

Back in Cleveland…

RICO.

Once Rico found out the location of West Side Bill, he was thirsty to put a bullet in his head. But like Gunner said, they were making too much money to jeopardize themselves, so he figured he would send a few of his goons. He put the play in motion, but first he had to hit Gunner up to make sure he called Richie Rich to make sure everything was a go on that end. Gunner picked up on the first ring. "What's up my nigga?" "I just put that one play in motion," Rico reported. "Did you ever call Richie Rich and set everything up? All we need him to do is find out is where Bill lays his head, and let him know we'll take 10 off each joint he buys,dx when he re-up." Gunner said "I'm on my way to the stash house, but soon as we hang up, I will call the Nigga." "Bet," Rico said. They chopped it for a few more minutes before they ended the call. Rico walked back into his master bedroom. Ashley was still laying across the bed nude. Rico looked her over and told her to get dressed. "I thought I was going to spend the day with you, she protested. "What made you think that?" he responded. She instantly caught an attitude, grabbing her clothes as she stormed off to the bathroom. "And hurry the fuck up!" Rico yelled.

Rico had a doctor's appointment. This was his second appointment since being released from the hospital. They wanted to make sure his lungs were healing properly. As he walked into the lobby of Metro, he saw Toya, his old head's wife. She was an R.N. there. They greeted each other. She gave Rico a respectable half hug and said "boy, you had us worried. You almost gave James a heart attack." Rico

laughed and said "my fault, but I'm good."
Toya said "let me get back to work. My break
is almost over, and I will tell James I bumped
into you today." Rico was seen and everything
looked good. They scheduled another
appointment in 30 days for a final follow-up.
He was glad to hear that his next visit would be
his last. He was already tired of coming back
and forth. He made his appointment because
his mother knew the doctor and he didn't feel
like hearing her mouth or adding any stress to
her. He had already given her one too many
gray hairs. He walked out of the hospital and
jumped in his new Jag truck he bought since
his q7 got shot up. He couldn't help it, he loved
to put on. He was headed to the hood to show
his face.

Chapter 17

TOYA.

When Toya clocked out, she called her husband James while walking to the car. He picked up on the third ring, "Hello." "Hey baby, you're just clocking out?" he asked. "Yes, they needed someone to help file the paperwork, and you know me, I ain't turning down no overtime," Toya replied. "Well, I was taking a nap while the boys were sleeping," James said. "How long before you get home? We miss you." Toya told James she had seen Rico at the hospital today. She told him she should be home within the next 45 minutes. She disconnected the call and blue-toothed her phone to the car so she could listen to music of her choice. She was jamming to Tyree *(Baby Won't You Just Stay)*. She regretted getting on the freeway. It was barely moving, so it took her an extra 15 minutes on top of the 45 minutes that it normally took. She pulled into the driveway and couldn't wait to get inside. She missed her babies and her big baby. Toya has been married for 17 years now, and James always made her feel like it was yesterday. No matter what, they promised to always give each other their all.

A Few Days Later…

GUNNER.

Gunner called Richie Rich a couple days ago to find out where West Side Bill lays his head. Today was his lucky day. He called Gunner with an address and let him know who all lived there. From the information he just gave him, it's just Bill. His baby mama fell through from time to time. Gunner ended the call and shot a text to 400. 400 and a few other young'uns were in the D camped out at a motel. They were waiting on the info I just sent. Play in motion after he made sure everything was in play, he called Rico. Rico told him he was leaving his old house and he would meet him in the hood. Gunner was parked sitting in his rental, and guess who came driving a Jag truck down the street - you guessed it, Rico, Gunner was shaking his head. He loved to see his n**** shine, but there is a time and place for everything. Gunner got out and walked up on the truck. Rico jumped out and started doing a little dance we call the Money Walk. I can't front, his comeback was definitely a statement maker. From a q7 to a brand new Jag truck with title in hand. This definitely let the streets know that he was alive and still getting to the bag. He saw the look on Gunner's face and said, "look dude, don't rain on my parade. I already know what you're thinking." Gunner didn't want to bump heads with his Nigga, so he just dapped him and gave him props, but he made a mental note to holla at Rico later about being so flashy. That is the reason a lot of dudes in the city went down, and he refused to become one of them.

RICO.

Rico heard Gunner loud and clear about being too flashy, but he wasn't trying to hit or s***. What's the point of getting money if you can't spend it? He wanted the city to know he was doing numbers. He drove through every Hood that was known for getting some real paper. He was the first nigga in the city to drive a Jag truck, and he cashed out. Boss niggas don't do notes. he said to himself just as he was turning onto 113th and Benham. He didn't do tint, so you knew who was driving. As he drove past the group of niggas standing alongside the sidewalk, there were a few nice whips out there. There was an AMG 17 Benz truck, a 460 Lexus, and a pretty ass Masi, but his Jag truck was the first one to be seen on Cleveland's streets. The guys were pointing as he drove past, and one even gave him the salute. He gave him a head nod in return, smiling like a kid in the candy store.

His next stop would be Politics in Maple Heights. Politics was a bar owned by this nigga Ress and his partners Jay and Shump. They had a nice set-up and some cold ass bartenders that gave it that sexy feeling. This kept niggas and females coming back. Rico pulled into the parking lot. There were maybe 10 vehicles in the parking lot. It was still early.

He backed his truck into the spot right in front of the door. There were a few people standing around the parking lot, and he knew all eyes were on him. He faked like he was scratching and adjusting his clothes, walking up to the bar. He was greeted by Boog and Tay, two brothers who were at the bar so much, you would have thought they owned the place. Rico took a seat at the bar. A bartender named Bianca came over and took his order. Salmon with glaze, lemon pepper wings and Hennessy with orange juice. He overheard one of the owners asking whose Jag truck was out there, "that bitch is aggressive," and the bouncer pointed down towards Rico.

Next Day…

WEST SIDE BILL.

Bill was still learning how the D operated. He met a few dudes here and there, he even ran into a guy he could re-up with once he figured out how to get some clientele and dump the remaining 200 grams he had left. He had been chopping it with these young boys that always stood outside one of the restaurants he frequented daily. He figured he would build a little squad and in that way he could purchase the pack and put it in their hands so he can make money without putting himself in harm's way. Also, he was still unfamiliar with his new territory. He planned to cut into the youngest in the next couple days. He just hoped he was making the right move. If everything went as planned, he would be back in the swing of things in no time.

He called his baby's mother and told her to meet him at his spot that evening. He had a surprise for her. The only thing he had for her was some dick. His baby's mother, being stuck on stupid, that's all he needed. If he said jump, she asked how high?

400.D.NELLE.

400, Tyson and Chris have been following Bill for two days. His routine was simple -- he comes out about 11:00 a.m., goes to a store about six streets from his building and he drives to a restaurant that is in the area where his baby's mother lives over by Seven Mile. He chopped it with the young boys before he entered, stayed for about 45 minutes to an hour, then shot over to his baby's mother's house and chilled there all day before he headed back home. He stopped at the same gas station every night. 400 figured this would be a cakewalk, so the play was put together to go down that night.

Later That Night…

400 and the young boys with him were ready. They were sitting in the car waiting for WestSide Bill to pull up. They knew the only way to get inside the building was to have the access card or be buzzed in after someone made a positive ID on the camera just above the door. So they planned to rush Bill as he walked into the entrance way. After waiting close to three hours, they finally see a familiar face. It isn't Bill, it's his baby's mother. They jumped out and speed walked in her direction. Just as she was using her key card to gain access, they roughly grabbed her and forced her into the lobby. They told her to take them to Bill's apartment if she wanted to live. They all got on the elevator. She pressed number four and they got off and headed down the hall to apartment 402. As they entered, 400 smacked her across her face and asked her where the money was. She was crying, saying she didn't know where it was.

400 told Tyson and Chris to check the bedrooms. He tied her up and began checking the living room. They figured they would clean out Bill before they murdered him. 400 was against it, but Tyson and Chris was thirsty so he said f*** Why not. As long as West Side Bill get his brains blown, Rico and Gunner will be pleased, and he and his niggas will be a couple hundred thousand dollars richer than before. No harm no foul, Tyson ran from the back

holding a duffle bag like Jackpot Bingo. 400 said "now all we got to do is wait for Bill to bring his b**** ass home." The young boy Chris was hyped. This was his first time seeing that much money, and a third of it was his, as he went to adjust his gun on his waist, it went off. Boom! Everybody was looking around like *what the fuck!* 400 began yelling. They heard moaning and gurgle sounds as if someone was hurt. When they looked towards Bill's baby's mother, they saw that a bullet had hit her in the chest area. 400 said "we got to bounce. Somebody definitely heard that gunshot and called the police. Fuck! was all 400 thought as they grabbed the duffle bag and ran out the door.

Chapter 18

Back In Miami…

PEDRO.

Pedro still had Margiela under the scope. His every movement was being reported back to Pedro. There hadn't been any more shootings or bombing attempts, but the tension was still present for all participating on both sides. Pedro planned to release some of his stress. He figured the best way was to hit up his favorite nightclub. He stopped by a few of his spots to make sure everything was running smoothly. After he had made his rounds, he went and got something to eat.

He and his driver were walking out of the Bodega as three sexy-assed ladies walked past, talking and laughing with one another. The three were identical. He could picture it now - him f****** all three at the same time. Just thinking about it had his manhood coming to life. He told his driver to wait as he slightly jogged to catch up to the triplets. As he was approaching, Tiff turned around and Tee and Lee did the same. He was smiling and couldn't believe it, he never fucked triplets before. He had a couple sets of twins here and there, but never triplets. He reached his hand out and introduced himself. "Hello, my name is Pedro; and what would you three beautiful ladies names be?" Each responded by giving him their names. "Tiff,Tee and Lee, what are you ladies doing later? I would like to invite you out tonight for a night of fun," Pedro offered. Tiff always being the one to speak for the three, exchanged info with Pedro and kissed him on the cheek. Tee and Lee did the same before they left. Pedro stood there and watched them until they were out of sight.

MARGIELA.

He had a gut feeling he was being watched, so he hired someone to follow him from afar, and sho nuff, he was being followed by one of Pedro's people. Now he knew he planned to let them keep following him and use this to his advantage. He was leaving one of the spots. The only place he didn't go to was to the Clubhouse. That was where the products were. There was also a large amount of cash stored there. He was en route to meet the Cash Money Chicks at their suite. As he pulled up to the hotel, he couldn't help but to smile. His little problem with Pedro would be no more in the next couple of days. He walked into the hotel and headed straight to the elevator. He got off on the 12th floor and walked to room 1206. He knocked twice, the door opened with Lee standing there smiling.

Margelia hadn't seen the triplets in a while, so yeah, they all were kind of happy in a way. He stepped into the room and got right to it. "I need y'all to hit this Latino muthafucka name Pedro. He is causing me hella problems." One of the triplets asked, "what did you say his name was, Pedro?" "Yes, and why do you ask?" Margelia questioned her. "Do you have a photo of this guy?" Tee asked. Margelia came ready. He pulled a few pictures out and handed them to the triplets. They all started smiling when they saw the photos. "This is going to be easier than we thought," Tiff said.

Margelia was lost, so they filled him in. "So I assume it is a go then, right? Because I need this dude dead like yesterday," Margelia said. "Don't worry about it. Cash Money Chicks are here to save the day," the ladies all said at the same time. They gave Margelia a hug and kissed him on the lips before he left. Once he was back inside his vehicle, he called Tiny to fill him in on the play he had just put into motion. Tony asked him to stop by. He wanted to holler at him about something important but not over the phone.

Time to Turn Up the Heat…

CASH MONEY CHICKS.

Tiff was just getting out of the shower. Drying off she observed herself in the full-body mirror. Tee had just stripped down to her birthday suit so she could jump in the shower. Lee had taken hers already and was doing her hair and putting on her makeup. Once the triplets were fully dressed, they were flawless. They called Pedro to let him know they were ready. Rather than send a car, he had his driver take a detour and picked them up personally himself. He was in awe when they came walking out of the hotel to his stretch Suburban limo looking like models on a runway. Inside the vehicle was a fully stocked bar and, of course, Pedro had a small bowl in plain view filled with some pure cocaine. He gave each lady a fluted wine glass and filled it with some very expensive champagne. They sipped on the bubbly and conversed while en route to the club.

Everyone had something on their mind, Pedro was thinking how sweet it was that these three sexy ladies would be all his by the end of the night after he slips the X pills into their drinks at the club. Tiff was already putting her plan into motion. She will be all over Pedro watching his every move. The only thing Lee was worried about was how she was going to fuck him before they killed him. Tee knew she loved to do coke, and there was a full bowl right in front of her. Pedro joined her and began to do lines also. It took them 40 minutes to reach their destination. The club was packed. The line was wrapped around the corner. When Pedro's driver pulled up to the curb, one of the doormen walked up to the back door and helped the ladies out first. Pedro followed. He and the triplets looked as if they could have been on the cover of Playboy. They were escorted inside and of course, they didn't have to wait in line. Pedro was well-known and he was good friends with the owner of the club. They were seated in one of the VIP areas.

It was going tonight. If you didn't know any better, you would swear it was a rave. The atmosphere was on fire. The triplets had every male in the building following their every move. They killed the dance floor while Pedro was in VIP getting wasted. Tiff sent a bottle of champagne to their section, but it was spiked with her secret potion that would give her full control over the situation tonight. She looked over at Pedro and blew him a kiss and stuck her tongue out in a nasty manner. He smiled with cocaine all over his nose. Tee was right by his side, and she licked it off. She put her head in his lap. It didn't take a rocket scientist to know she was sucking his dick. He had his eyes closed, head back with not a care in the world.

Four Hours Later...

They were in the back of the truck. Pedro was so out of it he didn't realize that while Lee was riding the f*** out of his dick, she held a small handgun with a silencer attached to the nozzle. Lee grinding her hips faster, faster, faster, she was chasing yet another nut. She had been f****** him for the last two hours non-stop. Her pussy was so wet a puddle began forming under Pedro. She brought her ass down with so much force it sounded like someone was clapping. Her orgasm was right there. She could feel it. She f***** him hard as she gripped his dick, and with the one hard thrust she exploded, letting out a moan. And removing herself off Pedro's dick she said to him "too bad all this good dick is going to go to waste." What she said registered in his brain because he opened his eyes to respond, but it was too late. She put a bullet into his left temple killing him instantly, or so she thought.

Chapter 19

MARGIELA.

Business has been booming ever since Cash Money Chicks did their thang. Margelia had Pedro put down; well somewhat. He wasn't dead, but he was lying in the hospital in a coma. The doctor said he was brain dead, but his family refused to pull the plug. With the leader out of the picture, the Looney Squad Mob had no choice but to roll with the program. The guy Pedro had following Margelia was kidnapped, had both of his eyes and his tongue cut out and released in front of one of their spots. He would never tell anybody what he saw and he would never see again. Margelia was so pleased with the demo the triplets put down, he asked them to stay in Miami for good. Shidd, they could take the place of that one group of females that was killing s*** in Miami a while back, but you know how it goes - new day, new blood (and three new pretty faces).

Lit Life was running through products like a kid eating candy. It was about time for another shipment. Margelia was headed to the diner to drop Julio the payment of 20 million cold cash. He was officially the new king of Miami. As he entered the diner, Julio was at his usual spot in the rear of the diner. Margelia approached carrying two duffle bags that were heavy as s***. He dropped them at the foot of the table. Julio greeted him, "how's it going my good friend?" Margelia answered, "it's going. Matter of fact, it's time I reloaded. I'm down to my last 20 kilos of H, and I've got only ten left of coke, so I'm going to need a loan ASAP, my friend." "Not a problem," Julio said. "I will put the order in right away. I will let you know when it is here, and you got it from there. Margelia thanked Julio for putting him in a position of power. "Don't mention it. Just as long as you know who has the real power." Julio said.

CHI CHI.

Chi-Chi received a call from Julio. The Miami District needs a shipment. Julio was right about the guy he picked to take over the Miami District. He ran through 200 kilos in 45 days. He liked the sound of that. He had to contact the driver to give him the details, "A load will be headed your way, my friend," Chi-Chi said as he ended the call. He called the farm and put the order in. Once the load is ready, he will call and text Trucker J with the pick-up location. He never used the same place twice in a six month's span. Chi-Chi looked over at his boss, Hector. They raised their glasses and both said cheers.

Back In Detroit...

WEST SIDE BILL.

Bill pulled up to his building. Police and homicide were everywhere. As he approached the doorway, an officer stopped him and asked "What apartment do you live in Sir?" "I live in apartment 402," Bill answered. The officer asked Bill to follow him and told him there had been a homicide connected with his apartment. Bill looked at the officer and said, "that can't be. I live alone." The officer asked if he knew a female by the name of Lisa Gray. His heart dropped instantly. He remembered telling her to meet him at his spot. "Yes, that's the mother of my son," Bill said with tears in his eyes. The officer asked Bill to identify the body. When he saw her, he flipped out. He went berserk. They had to restrain him and he was taken to the hospital. They believed he was in a state of shock. They kept him there overnight.

Once discharged the next day, he flew to his spot and went straight to the bedroom closet. Damn, his duffle bag was gone! He had $390,000 inside and it was gone. All he kept screaming was that he was fucked. He was flat broke, his baby's mother was dead, he had only two hundred grams left to his name, and he had to raise his son. Now was this a sign from God, or was this the devil trying to destroy him? Whichever one it was, he better make the right choice because this s*** is chess, not checkers, and he has no clue who put the play down.

400.

400 was pissed. He doesn't know how they fucked up. The move shit was going perfect; Chris was a young boy from his hood and he figured he would let him tag along just to put some money in his pocket. He knew Chris had never been on a mission like this before. Damn, he's got to come up with a story to tell Gunnar and Rico. He was on the freeway headed back to Cleveland. He was doing the speed limit because he couldn't afford to be

pulled over with a duffel bag full of drug money in the car. But he was no fool, so he made sure they got rid of the guns before jumping on the freeway. Now Tyson and Chris didn't give a f*** about not killing Bill. They were just happy with the duffel bag. Neither of them had ever seen that much money. Neither had 400. He was already putting a play together in his head. He was going to kill Chris and Tyson and keep all the money to himself. There is no honor among thieves. It was a quiet ride back with everyone in deep thought. They were getting off the freeway at East 55th. 400 said we can split this up at the one bando on 73rd and Cedar. Tyson and Chris said *cool*, never thinking they were in route to their own death. As they pulled into the backyard and parked, they all got out smiling. Chris and Tyson went towards the back door, but 400 said he had to piss and walked towards the garage. Once behind the garage, he grabbed a thirty eight that he hid there two years ago when he killed Jr. He put it on his waist and went into the house with Chris and Tyson.

As soon 400 walked into the dining room he shot Chris in the head. Chris never saw it coming. He was grabbing money out the duffle bag when his body hit the floor. The sound of the gunshot caught Tyson off guard. Being from the streets he went for his own gun on his waist, but remembered 400 made them throw the guns down a sewer drain before they left

Detroit. He was f*****. He tried to plead with 400, but it fell on deaf ears. He shot Tyson twice in the face then one more in the chest. He grabbed the money off the table and threw it back into the bag and bounced. He figured he would call Gunner in a few days and tell him the bad news about Bill getting away.

Back In Cleveland...

RICO.

Rico and Gunner were at Gunner's apartment in Bear Creek in Bedford. They were watching the news. Two young boys were found shot to death inside a vacant house on 73rd and Cedar. '*No suspects at this time. We will keep you updated.*' Rico looked at Gunner and asked "ain't that your young nigga 400's area?" "Hell yeah. He probably knew them little niggers too!" Gunner said. "Speaking of youngin ', have you heard anything yet?" Rico asked. "Nope, he's still down in the D. Trust me, soon as he flatlines that Nigga Bill, I will be the first person he calls." Rico chilled for a couple more hours before he went down to the hood.

Everything was running smoothly. They had s*** clicking. There was so much money being made Rico turned a few robbers into new hustlers, and they were getting to that bag in a major way. At first, n***** was leary to deal with them, but you can't deny what's already written, and the product was fire. Ever since he pulled his Jag truck out, the city has been talking. Them niggas getting some money down there on Fleet. Even the nigga Young Work from Benham was sliding through. Yeah, Rico was definitely putting on for his hood, unlike a lot of these n*****. He didn't just have a foreign car, he actually had the bag to match. Bitch was no longer a *thousandaire*, he most definitely joined the *Millionaire Boyz Club!*

He was en route to his favorite bar, Politics. He loved the salmon with glaze they served and he couldn't find any other bar that had it glazed. Like always, he ordered a Henny with orange juice and salmon with glaze and lemon pepper wings. He flirted with every female that came through the door. Shump, one of the owners, wanted to holla at him. At first Rico was spinning him, but he finally sat down and chopped it with dude. Come to find out Shump be bringing them bricks in, but lately his hook ain't been having shit good, so he was trying to f*** with Rico. Rico told him to give him a day or two and they could put something together, but first he had to make sure he was solid. We live in Cleveland and you never know who is working for the Fed.

Chapter 20

TOYA.

James just told Toya he had a run coming up in a few days and he would be gone for approximately two weeks. She was definitely going to make sure she got plenty of dick the next few days, starting today. She lay in bed under the covers messing with her pussy. The boys were at her mother's, so they would have the whole house to themselves. She waited until her pussy was nice and wet, then she got out of the bed and walked towards the kitchen.

In the kitchen, she bent over and acted like she was looking for something under the counter. She was ass-whole naked and her pussy was dripping. James was sitting at the kitchen table with the newspaper in front of him, but when she walked into the kitchen he couldn't take his eyes off that ass, and once she bent over, it was all she wrote! He got up and got on his knees behind her and stuck his tongue in her pussy. She let a low moan escape her mouth and she gripped his head as he ate her pussy from the back. Then he slipped his tongue in her ass. It was only right. She loved when he f*** her ass with his tongue. Once she busted her first nut, he stood up and pulled out his dick. It was rock hard and nine inches thick. She dropped to her knees and teased him; at first just licking around the head and up and down the shaft of his dick. In a flash she slammed it into her warm wet mouth, sucking hard and slowly as she looked into his eyes. That turned her on, staring into his eyes while she pleased him, and watching the faces he made, hearing him say "suck daddy's dick." She knew when he was about to nut. His dick would swell up and it would jump and pre-cum would spill out first. Then he would pump faster. She would swallow every drop, but sometimes she liked it to shoot all over her face when he nutted. He shot out thick milky white excrement when he nutted, and it had a salty taste that she loved.

After she sucked the nut out, they headed to the living room. He sat down on the sofa while she straddled him and slid right down on his dick. She stuck her tongue in his mouth, and he sucked on it. She began to f*** him hard and fast. She loved to fuck. That was one thing James loved about her. Her sex drive was through the roof. He grabbed her ass, spread her apart and thrusted upwards to meet her thrust. All you heard was bare skin slapping and her pussy noises, because she is coming back to back. James busted a huge nut inside her, but his dick was still rock hard because he had done a line of cocaine while she was upstairs. She doesn't know he plays with his nose, at least not yet. He flipped her and pulled her to him.   He spread her legs and put his dick up into her stomach she screamed "oh s***, this dick is good! Fuck me, fuck He. Give me all that dick!" They fucked for four hours straight. He had her pussy sore and lightweight swollen, and she still wanted more, so he went and snuck and did another line of coke. She was standing right behind him. "What is that?" she asked. He couldn't lie, so he told her the truth. She asked, "How does it make you feel?" He said "try a little and see," so she did a line and before you knew it, she was doing lines off his dick while he did lines off her pussy. Man, he created a sex monster, and they both loved it!

TRUCKER J.

When I opened my eyes, all I saw was ass and pussy. Me and the wife had a helluva night. There was a plate sitting on the coffee table with cocaine on it and a rolled up $20 bill. Me being me, I did a fat ass line, and my dick got hard right away. I walked over to where Toya was laying, knocked out with her legs wide open. One of our female friend's faces was buried between Toya's legs. Since I couldn't f*** Toya, I got behind China and eased myself down, putting my dick inside her ass and started grinding slow. She started moaning and began eating Toya's pussy. Toya opened her eyes and watched me f*** the s*** out of China's ass while China ate her pussy. It was good as f***. I pulled out and went to wash my dick. I came back in the living room to find Toya doing a line off of China's pussy, so I stuck my dick in her pussy and start f****** her like a madman. I pulled out, went and did another line, probably two, and Toya asked me if they could both do a line off my dick. I said "hell yeah!" After they did a line, they began to suck my dick. This session went on all day. A few nights later, we had another session, but it was far more freakier and more intense. I don't know if Toya would approve of me telling her about this night. We had plenty more after.

GUNNER.

Gunner heard through the grapevine that 400 was riding around in a candy red Infiniti truck on some forges. They must have cleaned Bill out before they downed him, he thought. He called 400 a few times but got no answer. He decided to slide through Cedar. He stopped at a bar called Wolf's Den. There was a candy red Infiniti sitting in the parking lot. He entered the bar, and the first person he saw was 400 with a lot of young boys all around him. You could tell he came into a couple dollars. He was rocking a hard Herman shirt with the belt to match, black slacks with some slip in loafers with the H on the buckle, a hard-ass Rolex flooded around the Bezel diamonds were definitely VVS's. His ears were chunky, a karat in each. He approached me and said, "I was just about to come your way. I lost my phone, so I had to buy another one.

What's good?" "What's the 411?" Gunner asked. 400 ran down the story and Gunner was pissed, but 400 looked up to Gunner and Rico, so he kept it a 100 by telling the truth. He told Gunner he would double back down to Detroit after it died down. Gunner was salty, but 400 was his little Nigga and he always came through. Shidd, Gunner thought to himself, I guess the saying is true you can't kill them all. The good thing about it is they took Bill's stash, so that means he's broke. That might force his hand for him to try and dip in and out the city to scrape up some paper. If he does come this way, he is a dead man walking. We already killed his baby's mother, so the next move is checkmate. He and 400 dabbed and Gunner walked out. 400 came out of the bar behind him and asked Gunner if he wanted part of the stash he grabbed. "How much was it?" Gunner asked. "$390,000," 400 answered. "Damn, West Side Bill was doing his thing! Naw youngin, that's all you. Remember, easy come, easy go so don't trust none of these n*****, and keep your business to yourself."

Chapter 21

TRUCKER J.

I just completed my run from New Mexico up to Miami. I love being out here on the road. It's a piece of mind, plus it pays well. I am on route back to the city $150,000 richer. Everything has been going smoothly and it's almost time for me to re-up. I've been thinking about having a sit-down with my young dude Young Work and see where his head is at. I think I'm going to fall back and let him control the ball. I will just pick up the load, transport it back and front Rico his usual. I will let Young Work run through the rest, but I can't front him. That's too risky on my end. I will sell him a kilo for $50,000 per key. That way, I will make $40,000 per unit. 200 kilos equals 10 million. I deduct two million for Chi-Chi and that leaves me with a cool 8 million every flip. I will call Young Work when I get back so we can make a plan to have a sit-down. One hand washes the other. S***, I have to take some time out one of my days, and count my money. I made so much money the last 12 months, I don't even know how much I have. I guess when you are getting real money it is easy to lose count.

Back In Miami

MARGIELA

We were just pulling up to Haitian Black's warehouse the same as the last time. Two 24-foot box trucks backed up to docks one and two. Margelia stood around talking shit with Haitian Black while the warehouse workers loaded the trucks. After the trucks were loaded, they headed across town to the clubhouse. Once they pulled up to the club house, he gave everyone their product to supply their areas, so each part was loaded and ready to rock and roll. It's crazy how months ago he was moving between 20 to 50 kilos, now he was running through 2000 kilos easily. But you know what they say, a boss is only as strong as his team. S***After the Cash Money Chicks took Pedro out of the loop, Tiny went full force in the areas they controlled. In a month's time Head Honcho, the Latino who took Pedro's place, started buying product from us. He figured it was better to make some money then no money, and eventually end up like Pedro. He's a smart man.

Margelia cleared 1.2 million and paid Julio and Chi-Chi. That left him with a 100 million. He took a loss here and there dealing with that Pedro beef, say about 1.5, give or take a few, but it was worth it. He removed 20 million from the safe behind the false wall. The two duffel bags were filled to capacity. He talked to a few of the Lit Life members before going towards the stairs that led to the second level. Once upstairs, it opened into a spacious six-bedroom condo. He planned to stop by the diner and drop Julio the 20 mil, so that way this load was already paid for. Once he is done with the shipment, it will put him and Lit Life in the range of 200 million, and this was just the beginning. He laid across the couch to take a little nap before he headed across town to see his good friend Julio.

CASH MONEY CHICKS.

Lee was always thinking about sex, and it didn't matter if it was with a man or a woman as long as she got to bust a few nuts. She was lying in her king size bed in the new condo she in the triplets just got, thanks to Margiela. They took him up on his offer and moved to Miami permanently. Of course, they still visited Cleveland on the regular. She was watching a porn on her 60 inch curved TV. She was fingering herself while she f***** her ass with a dildo the size of a baby's leg. She lay there for two hours doing all type of freaky s*** to get off. Her bed was drenched from the many orgasms she had. Her phone rang, but she was so into busting another nut, she never lost her rhythm. She rammed the second dildo into her pussy, fast and hard, over and over again until it became coated with her juices. She spread her legs and her toes began to curl. She felt it - it was right there. Just as she started cumming, her sister opened the door to ask her something, but she never noticed because she was moaning and groaning with her eyes closed. Her sister shook her head and close the door thinking to herself, *this b**** going to f*** herself to death one day!*

Lee just lay there for a while, sliding the toy slowly in and out of her pussy trying to savor the feeling, but all it did was get her going again and just like that, she was on her knees sitting down on the rubber dick she called Mr. Brown. She was riding it like a mad woman, ass going up and down, titties bouncing with every move she made. She nutted again, but wasn't ready to call it quits. She stood up and put one foot on the bed and slid it back up in her. It must have hit her G-spot because she squirted everywhere then fell on the floor, still cumming, and leg shaking like she was having a seizure. She lay there and fell asleep, dildo in her pussy and all.

45 Minutes Later…

Tee had been yelling Lee's name. I walked into Lee's room earlier and Lee was having a one-woman orgy, and from the looks of it, it appeared she was cumming that very moment. I shut the door and left her to it, shaking my head. That was almost an hour ago. Tiff and I were dressed and waiting on this freaky ass hoe. I went back to her room door, the porno still playing. She still can't be playing with her pussy. I hope she's in the shower and the porno is just still playing. I opened her door, and she is asleep on the floor with a dildo still in her pussy. Cum was running down her thighs, a large wet spot was in the center of the bed, and a puddle of her juices under her ass and pussy. The room smelled like she does this every day. I can't lie, the porno she had playing damn near made me go to my room and get one off. I woke her ass up and told her we were about to leave. Her Hand went right to the dildo and, you guessed it, she began sliding it in and out her pussy half asleep, moaning and grinding her hips. I slammed the door.

Tiff being the head of the group was already on top of her game and already putting a few plays into motion. She has been kicking it with this well-known young boy from Opa-locka that is getting a lot of paper. He has a nice mansion and he drives a Lambo, and he has a few other high-end cars. Tiff and Tee are on their way to have brunch with him. Tiff promised him that he could have his way with the three of them, but *Freaky Ass* is too busy masturbating and f****** herself into a coma. She does this from time to time, so today was not a good time. Tiff will figure something out. She always does.

In addition to the condo, Margelia also bought them three nice whips. Today they were driving the AMG Benz big body. They pulled up to the Young Hattin spot. It was a sight to see. He even had maids and had a few hands that took care of the grounds. They were greeted at the door by the doorman, or should I say woman. A very polite little old lady. She showed us to the back patio area. He had it set up really nice. A chef stood to the side. As we were shown to our seats, he pulled our chairs out for us. He's definitely a good catch. Too bad this is business and he's the paycheck that we will be collecting. We made small talk at first, then he got right to it. "I thought there were three of you," he said. "My sister is still at the salon getting her nails and toes done," I lied. "I didn't want to reschedule our date because I really wanted to see you. We can still have some fun. She is supposed to call me soon as she's done." We ate and drank, and you know what came next – yes, drugs, X pills, Molly, and of course cocaine.

I had never done coke a day in my life, but Tee was a Coke head and she loved to party. Before long, we were butt ass naked. They tricked me to try some X pills, so I did and before I knew it, I was doing lines off his dick and loving it. When we first arrived, it was just the young boy, but now it's like six guys. I'm high out of my mind, and every time one dick comes out my mouth, another is being put in. I can't protest because I was steady doing coke. I looked to my left and my sister is riding one guy while the other guys f****** her in the ass from the back. Before I knew what happened, I was in the same position. I never got f***** by two guys at once, but I tell you, it's mind-blowing! I think every woman wants to try it, they just don't know how and they are worried about what people might say. Shidd, to all women, you only live once. The same way you give your man a threesome, tell that nigga you want your threesome, and don't forget the Coke, X pills. We f****** and sucked until the next morning.

My pussy and ass were so sore. I was pissed and I feel like I got played. Tee just wanted to do more Coke, so we stopped by The Clubhouse on our way home to grab some from Tiny. I stayed in the car. I still couldn't believe we just got fucked by six dudes and the crazy thing is, I really enjoyed it and want to do it again. Once Tee finally returned to the car, I told her next time you suck dick, make sure you whip your face. She looked in the mirror. Cum was all over her lips and cheeks. She was so high she didn't feel Tiny shoot his load all over her face. Before we pulled off, I told Tee thanks for my new habit. She asked what's that?   I said cocaine and f****** two dicks at the same time, now open that shit so I can do a line.

Chapter 22

CHI-CHI.

Chi-Chi just received a call from Trucker J. He is ready to reload and he is paying the two million up front. Chi-Chi was pleased to hear that. He made a call to the farmers to let his workers know what he needed and where to take it for pick up. After he ended the call, he lay back in his office chair and took a sip from his glass. He had to make a trip to the states to pick up the 40 million from Julio who was surprised that Margelia paid for the shipment a week after it was sent to him.

He had other things on his mind. He and Hector were having some real problems with the Lamia cartel. Bodies were popping up everywhere. On both sides there was a war over power. After the take down of El Chapo, Hector felt he was the next big thing; but there was one man who didn't agree, and he was the head of the Lamia cartel. This is where it all started. Two bosses fighting for the top spot only equals mayhem and murder. I was headed to Los Lunas, New Mexico to pick up my load. Once I had my load secure, I was enroute back towards the City. It was going to take about two weeks, plus this is a personal run so I didn't get paid for it. I dropped the two million at the location Chi-Chi instructed me to.

Days Later...

I was pulling into the parking lot of Frederick's, a bar and grill located on Emery Road in Maple Heights. It is a nice spot to sit down and eat and have a few drinks. I was meeting Young Work there so we could discuss a few things. See, I figured I would lay the whole pack on him and give it to him for a lovely price. That way I eat, he eats, the City eats and everybody is happy. Well actually, I'm going to sell him 150 kilos for $50,000 a unit. The other $50,000 I'm going to front to Rico for $50,000 instead of the $70,000 I usually charge. Work was pulling up. He parked and entered the spot. I was seated at the bar ordering chicken alfredo and a double Hennessy with orange juice. He took a seat and placed his order. We sat for a couple hours and threw a couple back. We set a place and time for us to make the exchange. See, when dealing with this amount of drugs you can't trust anyone. I had him bring me the money first and then I told him where he could pick up the shipment. We dapped and went our separate ways.

I couldn't believe I just made 7.5 million off of one transaction; a 5.5 million profit in 20 minutes. Damn, life is good! I stopped by the house and put the suitcase in my stash spot. I left again right away because I still had to drop Rico the other 50 units. I will call him and tell him to meet me at my duck off spot. He pulled up, and we went inside. It was about 4:30 p.m. I was in a rush, and Toya had the boys waiting on me. My niece is graduating today and it starts at six p.m. at the Wolstein Center. I told Rico that my ex-partner said he was impressed at the rate he was moving the product, so he decided to hit him with 50 units instead of 20. Rico was like, "damn, I'm about to be the next Big Meech," and I corrected him "No, you are about to be the next Rico." Idolize a man never. I told him what was owed for this pack and he said no problem. He helped me get the boxes out of my trunk and put them in his car and I headed home. Just as I was getting off the freeway, my phone started ringing. When I looked at the screen, it was a name I hadn't seen or heard from in a minute. I answered, "what's up?" West Side Bill lightweight dampened my mood telling me his son's mother was murdered and they cleaned him out and he needed my help. I didn't even know he had a kid, but he is one of my youngins, so I definitely was going to throw him a lifeline.

YOUNG WORK.

There's a new sheriff in town, Young Work thought to himself. He just copped 150 kilos after he put two on it. He will have 450 kilos and would be able to bang them for $50,000 a unit. He will still make a 15 million dollar profit once he's done. He just spent 7.5 mil, but it was well worth it. This new deal he has with Trucker J has put him in a way better position.

He bought three houses on Benham so he could have a cut house, stash house and a money house and each served a purpose. His whole team was shooters. Before they dabbled in the dope game, they were all robbers, and there was unity in their hood. One for all and all for one, and they stood on that. His team did numbers, but now they were flooding the City and had niggas coming from out of town to cop. Cleveland was usually the buyer, but times have changed. Now Cleveland was a main hub to cop kilos of H, the section from the East 116th and Buckeye area was a gold mine, and East 131st and Lenacrave was always going. From 94th to 114th and Miles was going, then you got 105th to 103rd and Union definitely getting their piece of the pie. 93rd and Myra was going stupid. Brothers, Luke and Tone had that b**** looking like a 24-hour drive-thru. 116th and Kinsman niggas retire and invest their money into dump trucks. Everybody knew it was something special about those brothers. We called them the two-headed snake.

Young work was standing among a few other guys. He put 30 kilos in his one nigga's hand, 30 kilos in another's hands, and 40 in his one nigga hands. That's 100 units he has out in the streets. He ain't worried about his team. They were one of a few who played by the rules in this slimy ass game. The only way they played foul was if you crossed one of them, or you ran off with the pack, but Work had no problem putting that s*** in the street. His nigga Mojizzle just got knocked up and had to take a cop for 18 years in the Fed. Before that happened, Mojizzle was putting on for the city. He was from 116th and Kinsman, but he and Work had teamed up and did numbers. Damn, the streets are going to miss Mojizzle for sure. The sun was going down, so you know that meant it was time to get ready for the club. They all jumped in their cars and went home to get fresh. You knew when Benham was in the spot. It looked like a video shoot – 30 deep and every last one of them got a bag on them. They are the Cleveland BMF, real talk! The parking looked crazy. You name it, it's out there.

RICO.

Rico and Gunner were sitting on a few million, and after they run through this shipment they will be worth 18.5, give or take a few hundred thousand. Of course, they put a two on it and they had niggas paying $100 a gram. That is $100,000 a kilo. They heard them n***** had it for $50 a gram, which is $50,000 per kilo, and it was the same s*** they had. Rico figured his old head people were supplying them as well, but Rico wasn't tripping. He had his own clientele in the City and hella out-of-towners. Paper hating was not in his blood. He loved to see real niggas getting to the bag. It was the hoe ass n***** he felt shouldn't have any money; niggas who snitched shouldn't be allowed to own s*** , flat out.   But these n***** be quick to say he didn't tell on me, or that nigga got the pack. Okay he got the pack, but he's a snitch. We don't spend money with hot niggas, we take that shit. In the Fed, hot niggas get run up top.

Everything was flowing. One of my young boys introduced me to this crazy ass white boy from the West Side named Lenny. He was grabbing five at a time, he just was reckless than a muthafucka, but I overlooked it because $500,000 is a lot of paper. Like any other day, I was on Fleet doing what I do best, getting to the bag, and I stopped driving my personal wheels through the hood. Gunner was in my ear about us opening up a club and restaurant. Lately, he has been on some. He is ready to go legit s***, I can't lie, the Feds have been tearing the city up, but there is too much money to be made, and I feel like Fifty Cent, I'm going to *get rich or die trying*.

WHITE BOY LENNY.

Lenny had no clue that he was being followed by the Feds everyday. It all started 18 months ago, due to a few overdoses, four were fatal, and all fingers pointed in his direction. He was already on the radar for heavy drug activity and several shootings, but once those overdoses came into play, it brought the Feds into the picture. Like they say, once the Feds get onto you they don't stop until they get you. See, they knew Lenny was a pawn in the chess game. If they put enough pressure on him, they knew they could get him to flip, and sho-nuff the Feds had a trick up their sleeve. Lenny was sitting on his couch on 73rd and Colgate. The street was full of life. Junkies were everywhere, drug dealers out in the open making hand-to-hand transactions, and you guessed it, the Feds were in the utility truck down the street taking pictures and recording.

It was just a matter of time before they would round Lenny and his flunkies up for the slaughter. One of the agents said "I think it's time we send our guy in. See if we can get him on the inside." "It's your call," another agent said. "First thing in the morning get him assigned to this case. He's a young wild agent, rough around the edges, but that's just what we need. He will fit right in, and he played a big role in taking down those brothers who ran the Black Mafia family. That was a huge case, one for the records. Let's call it a day. These dumb fucks will be out here tomorrow. They think this s*** is legal. Wait hold up! Who is that pulling up in that f******* Impala? Get a photo of him and run those plates." Lenny walked towards the rental Rico was sitting in, and he stuck his head into the passenger window. They talked for a few minutes and Rico pulled off with no clue the Fed just took his picture.

Chapter 23

GUNNER.

I was just leaving a building I was interested in leasing or buying to open my Club. I ran it by Rico, but he didn't want to invest. Rico was my right-hand man, but we have different goals. Every hood nigga wanted to be the next Scarface, but we all see how that movie ended.

This is the perfect time for us to get into something legit. We have some real money put up, and number two, the Feds have built new headquarters downtown. It doesn't take a rocket scientist. Yeah, we came a long way but it's only a matter of time before the ship sinks. There are three ways to leave the game. You can be driven away in a casket, you can get hauled off in handcuffs, or you can walk away a free man on your own terms. I refuse to be one of those you hear in the hood about how dude was balling and dude getting to the bag, but dude got life or they killed dude cause they were hatin. When they tell my story, they are going to say "dude is up and got out, now he owns a few clubs and a few other things. I just can't get my nigga Rico to transition with me. I feel like it's going to cost him everything that he grinded so hard for.

One thing I have learned is to always go with my gut feeling, and there is something telling me that the white boy Lenny ain't right, but Rico won't listen to me. The building I just looked at seemed perfect for what I want to do. My older dude, Mad is like Ghost off Power. He owns well-known clubs and a restaurant that's doing really well. He has been doing this forever. It seems like forever, so I went to him for some advice as to how to properly get a club up and running. He had no problem giving me the blueprint. He said that first, you have to be hands-on with every aspect from the interior design down to the recipes you're going to use for the menu, and finally and most importantly, is making your establishment a safe and friendly environment. He wished me good luck and said if I ever needed some information not to hesitate to give him a call. I pulled off from Mad's restaurant, The Broiler feeling good. I knew opening the club was going to be a challenge, but nothing worth having in life comes easy. I was more than ready. I left the West Side full of life. I had a vision even if no one else saw it. One thing for sure, they are definitely going to see the whole picture once I'm done painting this masterpiece.

WEST SIDE BILL.

Bill was mentally fucked up about his son's mother Lisa getting killed. He didn't eat for days. He couldn't sleep and he was so out of it, his son had to stay with his mama for a few weeks. Once he realized this was not a nightmare, he got himself together and made a few phone calls. One call was to his old head, Trucker J. He knew he could reach out to J for a little help. He still couldn't believe all of his money was gone. It took him years to save that kind of paper. He was so mad at himself for being stupid and keeping all his bread in one location. That type of money should have been split up and stashed in different places.

"F***" was all he kept saying. He called his Mom and told her he was about to pull up. He picked his son up and they went for ice cream. His son kept asking for his mommy, but he couldn't find the words to explain the situation. It was crushing Bill, even though he wasn't with his baby's mother. He loved her so much and he didn't get to tell her, and now he will never be able to. Seeing his son looking sad and lost lit a fire inside of him. Whoever killed his son's mother will pay for it with their lives, Bill thought to himself. After he and Junior were done with their ice cream cones he dropped him back off at Lisa's mother's house. He told his son he would pick him up on Monday after he got out of school, and to have all his stuff packed, because he will be living with him from now on. Junior was happy. He said "I will be waiting and ready Dad," and ran off to his room.

Bill told his mom he had to handle a few things, and that he would be back on Sunday night. He had to shoot out to Cleveland. She gave him a hug, and said "baby, you be careful out there. All Junior has left is you. I'm getting old. He needs you more than ever now Billy," She said, using his whole name. He kissed her on the cheek and said "I know." Bill was en route to Cleveland to holla at his old head Trucker J. He had no clue that Rico and Gunner were behind his son's mom being killed, but he knew they were still looking for him, because he kept in contact with a few people from the City.

Once he made it to Cleveland, he called Trucker J. He told him to stop by the house. As he pulled up, Toya and the twins were sitting on the porch. Trucker J was doing his barbeque, getting the grill going. It ain't a weekend that J don't barbeque. "What's up old man?" Bill said as he approached him. They hugged and laughed. He asked Bill how he was holding up. Bill told him "mentally I'm lost. It feels like I lost a part of me, and my son still doesn't know yet." "How do you tell a little boy that his mother is never coming back? Damn, it's crazy how life can throw you a curveball when you least expect it." "Well, you know I got your back," Trucker reassured him. "What do you need? You name it, it's yours." Bill said "just a few dollars to get me back up and running." "Not a problem," Trucker said. "Give me a few minutes. Let me run in the house and put something together for you."

When J came back out he was carrying a duffle bag and handed it to Bill. It was heavy. Bill asked "what is this?" and J said "there is $300,000 there. Look, these streets will swallow a man's soul. Take this cash and go be the father your son needs you to be, Promise me you will walk away from the streets and never look back." A tear ran down Bill's face as he embarrassed his old head. They discussed life for a couple of hours, had a few drinks and then Bill was back on the freeway headed to Detroit to be the man he needed to be for himself first and then for his son. The money Trucker J gave him was a second chance at life, and he refused to waste it.

TRUCKER J.

I was sitting in my den reading one of my favorite books, "Forty Eight Laws of Power." Thinking about a few things, I watched Bill grow up. His old man and I go way back. He was a good kid, he just got sucked into the streets and hung around the wrong crowd; but overall, he was a good kid. I just hope he heard what I said. These streets don't have love for anybody. They will build you up and if you don't make the right choices, they will take it all back. I was brought out of deep thought by the sound of my phone ringing. It was Rico. I answered, "What's going on youngin?" Rico said "Shit, I was just calling to tell you I would drop that to you in the morning for you to give to your people. Man, this shit got the city teed which means turned." "That's what's up" I said, "but I'm going to be at the gym in the morning. Meet me at Lifetime on Richmond off of Harvard. Matter of fact, just put it in my truck then call me so I can lock my doors." "Bet, said Rico. I ended the call and picked up where I left off in my book."

Chapter 24

HECTOR

Shit just hit the fan back in Mexico. Chi-Chi
was ambushed by the Lamia Cartel. Hector
was just notified about the attack. Chi Chi was
caught coming out of his favorite Bodega
eating a burrito. He said a man walked up and
shot him over 15 times before jumping into a
red Jeep and fleeing the area. To everyone's
surprise, he survived. He was in critical
condition, but the doctor said he would pull
through, no main arteries or organs were hit so
he is very lucky. Hector had around the clock
armed guards placed inside and outside Chi-
Chi's hospital room. He wasn't taking any

chances. He even had armed guards spread throughout the parking area watching entrance points.

One thing for sure, Hector was about to send a message to the head of the Lamia cartel. Hector always prepared for the worst. He had some people find out what school the kids of the head of the Lamia cartel attended. At this very moment, the head of the Lamia cartel, El Rosso's children were being kidnapped. They will be held for ransom, and once the money is delivered, Hector will deliver his children back to him piece-by-piece. No one really knows Hector's background. He came from a poor family and had to grow up fast. He himself earned everything he's ever gotten. He murdered and killed his way to the top. He might be the boss, but he still loves to get his hands dirty, or should I say bloody. If war is what Lamia wants, then war is what they shall have.

EL ROSSO

El Rosso's wife called him. She was hysterical, crying uncontrollably and yelling into the phone. He was trying to understand her, but he couldn't comprehend what she was saying. Someone else got on the phone and delivered the devastating news that rocked El Rosso's world. His children have been snatched and a ransom note was sent with the amount of 200 million being demanded. See, in this underworld they live in, it's a dog-eat-dog world. He knew in his gut that his kids were good as dead, but his father instinct is telling him to pay the ransom. He told the person on the other end of the phone to get the money ready and then hung up. El'Rosso was so focused on taking over, he made the fatal mistake of not looking at the chessboard from every angle, and now his kids will pay with their lives.

When he pulled up to his estate, it looked like a funeral was taking place. Family members were everywhere and mostly all the females huddled around his wife crying. As soon as she laid eyes on her husband she went berserk. He stood there and let her get it all off, then grabbed her and held her while she cried in his arms. He had to wait for instructions from Hector, the boss of the Aztec cartel. He prayed that he gets his kids back in one piece. Still no call from Hector. This was torture.

Back In Cleveland…

RICO

Rico was making his rounds. This was his fourth time dealing with white boy Lenny, and every time he dealt with him, he was being watched. See, Lenny was under investigation going on two years now, so I guess you can say Trucker J made the right choice by cutting all ties with the crazy white boy from the West Side. However, Rico had no clue and neither did Lenny, but his world was about to come crashing down. As Rico pulled up to his last drop off, his right-hand man Gunner called and told him to meet him at Scorchers, a sports bar located on Miles Road in Bedford. Everywhere Rico went, a Federal agent was tailing him and taking pictures of every person he came in contact with. Good thing Gunner was already at the bar inside. The agent couldn't leave his car and follow Rico inside. He didn't want to blow his cover.

As Rico entered, he looked around in search of Gunner and his youngin, 400. They were sitting at a table eating wings and talking. Once he was seated, Gunner got right to it. "We came a long way and made a lot of paper. I'm about to open up a club and a restaurant." Gunner said. "That's not all. I'm done with the game. I'm walking away for good. It just doesn't feel right no more. I outgrew it. I want something different, and I want to be free and alive to enjoy it." "So you just going to leave me out here dolo? I thought you were my brother," Rico retorted. "I am but you don't want to listen to me, so I gotta do what I feel is best for me." Gunner said. "You're going to always be my right hand, I just can't do this anymore. I ain't leaving you out here dolo, 400 is going to step into my spot. I've been teaching him ropes these past few months. He's ready and he's loyal, but you already know that. There is, 18 million in the stash. I'm grabbing my half and I'm out." Gunner said. Rico wasn't feeling it, but he had to respect it. His nigga wanted better, plus had the common sense to do what every drug dealer wishes they did - walk away on your own terms. "Cool," Rico said. He looked at 400 and said "You ready to get rich?", 400 responded saying "Let's get this paper Big Homie."

Rico told 400 to meet him at the stash spot in the morning before he bounced out. Rico was going to move his nine million someplace else before 400 ever made it over to the spot. Gunner had removed his money from the stash house a few days ago. Rico pulled out of Scorchers parking lot and you guessed it, the Federal agent was right behind.

GUNNER

Gunner was in the kitchen of his Club taste testing some of the dishes that were on the menu. Today was a special day - the renovation was complete, the kitchen staff had the kitchen smelling good and he had a selected group of close friends and family coming through to see the finished results and to enjoy what he had created. The setup was upscale, but he didn't overdo it. At the entrance, the front door was a VIP section, on the right, an all-white sectional with silver and glass tables, non-breakable glass and royal blue carpet. A spacious dance floor opened up just past the VIP section with one wall covered with mirrors and a door on the opposite wall. Behind the door was a nice sized kitchen. Just past the dance floor was a bar to the right. The bar seated 25. Three televisions hung overhead opposite the bar and there was a fish tank built into a brick wall that held a few Oscar fish in the tank. The tank set the bar area off. There is a more secluded VIP section for individuals who want more privacy.

Two Cleveland off-duty police officers will work the doors for days that the Club is expected to be packed. There will be two bouncers in place, and they have licenses to carry firearms. Everything's in place now it's time to get the money. Family and friends began to arrive around 4:30 p.m. Everyone was congratulating Gunner on the overall outcome. He thanked everyone for coming out. He told his guests, "I really appreciate you, and let's enjoy the evening." As he stood back and watched the flow of things, he couldn't help but think "*I used to pay to get in clubs and now I own one.*

*Damn, I wish my nigga Rico would have just
listened to me just one time.*"

400

400 was having his way. Rico and Gunner had
put him on a whole 'nother level. He was
putting so much heroin on Cedar niggas
thought it was the late 80s and early 90s again.
Back then a guy named Wilert made millions
right out of a record store that was there back
in the day. Rumor was he ended up turning
into a hot nigga. Damn, it's been a few months
since Gunner called it quits. 400 went from
being a shooter to supply n***** all over the
city. Rico wasn't really feeling him though.
400 was young and hard to control, especially
since his new position put him into a little
power and some real money. He was doing
s*** his way, not meeting Rico when he called
for a meeting (which was a good thing since
the Feds were following him).

400 was just pulling up to the store on 79th and
Cedar, to meet one of his drops. He upgraded
from the Q Infinity to an all white Masi. Yeah,
he was on his Yo Gotti s***. No forges, he was
getting his grown man on for sure. He didn't
really have that many problems. He was well-
known for being a young wild nigga that had
no problem airing s*** out at the drop of a
dime, and he brought all his young n***** along

for the ride. His squad was a bunch of young robbers and shooters that dressed and drove whips that would make you think they were heavy in the game. S*** them niggas didn't sell not one gram. Their only job was to protect the bag, and 400 was the new bag. He even changed his name to New Bag. He had everybody calling him that s***.

His nigga Dude pulled up just as New Bag was about to dip. "Damn Nigga! Why you always have a Nigga sitting around waiting like this s*** legal?" "My fault, my phone was going stupid," Dude said. "Next time you have me waiting, I'm going to make you chase me all over the City for your pack. Let's see how your phone jumps then. This shit way stronger. Put a three or four on it before you put it on the streets," New Bag said. Dude reached to grab the book bag off of the passenger seat floor, then handed it to New Bag through the window. "How much is this?" "A hundred thousand," Dude answered. "Cool, there are three units in the Villa bag in my trunk. Make sure you close my trunk all the way this time, and you owe me two Large. Get at me when you're done." New Bag said before pulling off.

Chapter 25

Back In Miami…

JULIO

Julio was wondering why Chi-Chi never came to make the pickup, and he wasn't answering his phone. Julio had no clue what had happened back home in Mexico until he received a call from his boss, Hector. Chi-Chi was in the hospital, but there was still business that needed to be handled, so Julio was instructed to return to Mexico right away. He made a call to Margelia to have him meet him at the diner immediately. He wanted to inform him that he personally would be leaving the states for a month or two. Everything would still run as if he was there, and if he was needed to just call. The shipment would still be delivered to the same location, and Haitian Black knew what was going on.

Julio was walking towards one of his many cars. Unlike Chi-Chi, Julio didn't use a driver. Even though he was an underboss, he liked driving himself around, so if there was an attempt on his life, he felt better being behind the wheel. That way his life was in his hands and not someone else's. He chose the Viper. He loved the look, and if he felt any danger nearby, the power this car put out would definitely get him out of harm's way.

Traffic was terrible due to an accident on the highway. He finally made it to the diner. Margelia was already waiting inside. Julio had never seen him drinking coffee and reading the paper. He also noticed another change in Margiela. He dressed down in more modest suits. He was growing into his role as a boss. After the meeting with Margelia, he headed to the airport. He called ahead for someone to contact his pilot to have the jet ready for takeoff. Just like that, he was up in the air, sipping on Brandy and on his way to his homeland, Mexico. He loved the states, and when he was sent to the states to oversee their money and product he was happy, so for them to be sending for him, things must be really bad back home, he thought.

CASH MONEY CHICKS

The triplets had been on their game. Tiff finally pulled off the move she had been working on for the past month or so, and it was worth it. She had been having threesomes with that young Haitian and his boys for the past two months. Coke and dicks have started to become a habit. She would do some coke and instantly, she wanted to f*** two niggas at the same time. Yeah, she f****** a few women also, but it was something about two big dicks at the same time. One time she was riding the young Haitian nigga and his friend got behind her and put his dick into her pussy too. She literally had two dicks in her pussy at the same time, and they were fucking the soul out of her. It was mind blowing, and now she craves those types of demos.

She finally pulled it off. They hit for seven mill. He had it in a walk-in closet the size of a living room. He had a walk-in safe. They tortured him for four days, but he still refused to open the safe, so they killed him. But you know Lee's freaky ass sucked his dick until it got hard and fucked him before she put a bullet in his head. She has issues. The triplets had been spending a lot at the Lit Life Clubhouse. It had a nice setup and the bar was one of the coldest in Miami. They started seeing less of Margiela, and when he fell through to show his face, he is wearing suits all the time now.   I guess when you're raking in millions that is the attire for a boss. Tiff had a gut feeling that before the night was over, she would be somewhere with two dicks and a pile of coke. She couldn't help it, she was addicted.

HEAD HONCHO

Head Honcho was doing business with Lit Life MC's because he felt he didn't have a choice. If you can touch his boss in his mind, you can touch him, but he kept telling himself he would get revenge for the attempt that was made on Pedro's life. They have him lying in a coma. Many don't know that Honcho isn't just Pedro's second-in-charge, he is his son. Honcho is at the hospital every day and he sits and talks to his father. "Dad, I know you can hear me and I know you are a fighter. You took out the most feared Haitian cartel in the United States, so I know you are not laying down to no pussy black muthafuckin Motorcycle Club. I know you're just laying here getting rest, and I know you hear me. I know you are going to wake up, and that is why I refuse to cut the machine off. I'm here, and I'm going to be here until you open your eyes. You hear me?"

At that moment Pedro squeezed his son's hand. He couldn't wake up, but somehow he heard every word his son said, and all he could do was squeeze his hand. Head Honcho just looked down at his father Pedro smiling. He knew it was just a matter of time before his father woke up. He walked out of the hospital formatting a plan that would make his father proud. He had already done his homework, and he found out that the Cash Money Chicks were the ones who pulled the trigger. They were living on borrowed time and didn't even know it.

Chapter 26

WEST SIDE BILL

Bill was sitting on a bench at the park watching his son interact with the other children. He took his old head's advice and relocated to Atlanta to make a fresh start. He took $100,000 out of the $300,000 Trucker J gave him. He opened a barbershop, bought a nice house for $125,000, and he put $50,000 in a bank account for his son. By the time his son turns 18, with interest, it will have increased to $115,000. He put the remaining $25,000 into a bank account in his name. He had equity in his barbershop and his home. He was in the process of building his credit, which he figured he might need one day.

He made sure he kept in touch with his old head Trucker and he was also trying to get Lisa's mom to move to the A. He wanted to put her in a nice place of her liking, but she declined. He would fly her in to visit whenever her or junior missed each other. You know Lisa is smiling down from heaven. Damn, he missed her so much. Why did it take losing her life for him to break the chain of events. The sound of his son's voice brought him out of his deep thoughts. "Daddy, you ready to go get some ice cream? I'm going to buy you some ice cream okay? I got four dollars." Bill couldn't help but laugh. He picked his son up, swung him around in a circle and hugged him tight. The normal life isn't all that bad. It felt good not to have to look over his shoulder. After work, he enjoyed relaxing around the house. Now, all he wanted to do was live.

FEDERAL AGENT WALLACE

Mone had been sliding through 73rd and Colgate for a month now. He was trying to make his face familiar around the neighborhood. He even had a few people meet him in front of Lenny's crib because he wanted Lenny to see him hitting a few drops. That way, he will think he is a part of his world. Just as he hoped, Lenny approached him at a gas station one day, but it wasn't until they bumped into each other at the strip club Ledos that Mone bought 500 grams from Lenny. Lenny wanted to make sure Mone knew how much he was booming. He bought the bar out for the night and again the following day, saying if you can't pay for it twice then you shouldn't be doing it.

Mone had been to the house on Colgate was now in the loop. Lenny also had an apartment on 64th and Detroit. He said that was just a place to stash work and money. Mone played his role so tough Lenny asked him if he could give him a kilo of H to get rid of somebody for him. Things were working out better than he expected and Mone couldn't believe it. He was acting like he was thrown back so he fed Lenny some b******** and Lenny bit the bait. He said he wanted a guy called Trucker J killed. Lenny was still pissed that Trucker J cut him off, which caused him to lose a lot of money. Mone had gathered enough evidence to arrest and charge Lenny with things that would get him a life sentence unless he agreed to work with the Feds. After Mone was out of Lenny's eyesight, he made a call to other agents to start rounding up Lenny's crew and raid every spot that he runs or has ever stopped before doing any form of dealings. He wanted a few agents sent to the location he and Lenny had been to so the other agents could make the arrest and his cover wouldn't be blown. So the takedown begins.

WHITE BOY LENNY

Lenny was engaged in a conversation when the Federal agents walked up on him. He made big ass commotion as he was being dragged out and hauled downtown to the Fed building. He was already willing to cooperate with the Feds before they even had him inside the interrogation room. Yes, crazy ass White Boy Lenny ain't as crazy as everyone thought.

As soon as he was placed inside the small room with the two-way mirror, he began to tell it all. The Feds have a 98 percent conviction rate, because of snitch-ass niggas like Lenny who get caught, and instead of taking their hit like a stand-up guy, they tried to save their own ass by bringing others down. Guys like Nicky Barnes, John Gotti Hitman, Sammy the Bull, and that rat ass nigga Alpo made niggas feel like it's okay to take other men's freedoms. After he was interrogated for six hours, they knew everything about Rico, and I mean everything.

Lenny was transported to CCA in Youngstown Ohio. He would be there from about six months to a year. He was processed, changed out into a jail uniform, and assigned to a pod. It was late when he finally made it to his pod. All he wanted to do was get some sleep. He would jump on the phone first thing in the morning when they pop their doors. His main focus was getting into PC, because he heard stories about niggas getting stabbed up for cooperating. He knew eventually the word would get out, so he would be walking on eggshells.

RICO

Rico walked into his condo in downtown Cleveland that he had rented just a month ago. He was downtown so much at the Casino and clubbing that he decided he might as well look into leasing an apartment downtown. As soon as he placed his keys on the coffee table, his door came crashing in. "Get down!" the FBI ordered. Rico never kept anything in his personal home, so he wasn't worried about them finding anything. He was cuffed while they tore the place up. The only thing they would find was the $300,000 he made today. He didn't get around to dropping it off at the stash house, so it was in his bedroom closet. It hit him that someone must be telling for the Feds to be raiding his crib.

Once they got him down to headquarters and into one of the interrogation rooms, an agent walked in and started the long process. Rico never broke or folded. His only words were "Can I get my lawyer?" The agents looked at each other and started laughing. "Sure you can have your lawyer." One of the agents even handed him his cell phone. This is not a state case. You have graduated to the big leagues. Rico couldn't believe his whole world was crashing down all around him. He thought of his nigga Gunner. Damn, he should have listened to his nigga. Rico was tired and fed up with the whole process. He told them to take him to CCA so he could get comfortable.

After he was processed and classed to a pod, he was headed to the same pod that White Boy Lenny was on. When he entered the pod, Lenny was in his cell so he had no clue that Rico had just arrived. Rico dropped his shit at his cell and jumped on the phone and called Gunner. Gunner picked up when he heard a collect call from a Federal holding facility at CCA. Rico started off by telling him to contact his lawyer and his old head and tell him the Feds snatched him up. "I believe somebody is cooperating and giving up info," Rico said. "Damn" was all Gunner could say. He would never kick his nigga while he's down by saying *I told you so.* He just held it in. "Okay I will send somebody to load your books and set up a number so you can call and get straight through. No telling how long they going to have you sitting in that b****, and don't worry, I'm riding with you until my casket drops," Gunnar said. "Hey, go to you know where and grab that and put that money up for me," Rico instructed Gunner. "Use some to open some more clubs and restaurants. I wish I wasn't so f****** bullheaded and had listened to you, my Nigga, but I made my bed now I got to lay in it. As soon as we get off the phone, call my old head up. Oh, and take 2.5 out my money and get it to my old head. Free or locked up, I've got to keep my name good." "I got you my nigga, and I will have that number for you to use as a burnout line. Stay up," Gunner said.

Just as Rico hung up the phone, he spotted a face that he knew. It was White Boy Lenny walking out of the pod heading to the lunchroom. They had just called chow. When Rico finally walked into the lunch room it was jam-packed. He saw niggas from all over the City. *Damn, this where they been hiding niggas*, he thought. He spotted people he f*** with real heavy; other faces were just faces he knew from clubbing and kicking it. When he spotted White Boy Lenny, he couldn't even look Rico in the eyes. He turned away like he didn't see him. Rico called his name and he looked his way and threw his hands up like 'what's good.' Rico said "Shidd, you tell me." They got their food, sat across from each other and talked until it was time for the next pod to come out to eat. Lenny was nervous and fidgety, and once they were headed back to the pod, he said he had to go to Medical. Later that night, Rico asked somebody where Lenny's cell was, because he hadn't seen him since the lunchroom. A skinny white dude said they moved him because he said he was scared his co-defendant might find out he's telling on him. Rico asked the white boy if he knew who Lenny's co-defendant was, the white boy said "yeah, he said it was you."

Chapter 27

TRUCKER J

Toya came down the basement stairs holding my phone out to me. "Someone named Gino is on the phone," she said. I became worried because Gunner never used his government name. I grabbed the phone, "What's going on Youngin? "The Feds snatched Rico and hit all the spots. They didn't find drugs. The only thing they found was $300,000 at Rico's condo downtown, but he said he thinks somebody is telling," Gunnar said, "and oh yeah, he told me to drop them little ends off to you too." "Damn the Feds. That means that they could have been watching for some time now," I said. I was panicking. "Calm down Old Head, if they have been watching us, me and you wouldn't be having this conversation," Gunner said reassuringly, "We would be in CCA with Rico. Trust me, I think it's that white boy from the West Side that is working with the Feds." "What white boy from the West Side?" I asked. "This crazy ass white boy named Lenny from 73rd and Colgate," he answered. I couldn't believe my ears. "Are you sure he was f****** with dude"? "I'm positive. That's one of the reasons I walked away and opened my clubs and restaurants. Dude used to do hot s***, and hot shit equals jail, but Rico kelp f****** with him because he was spending $500 to a million at a time. Rico overlooked all the red flags and sold his soul for the paper." Gunner said. "S*** this s***crazy. Look, I know you're out the game, but I need you to make sure that young boy Rico f****** with, closed up shop for a while. We've got to figure out what's going on. "Ain't shit to figure out. That white boy telling, and my young boy 400 is smarter than you think," Gunner said. "Alright, meet me at the Giant Eagle on Warrensville Center and Libby so I can grab them, few dollars. I will be in my Cargo Van.

400.

400 also known as New Bag was out and about making rounds when one of his young boys called him and said they ran up in all the spots on Fleet, but they didn't find anything. The people who were at the house said it wasn't vice, it was the Feds. New Bag told his young boy to close up shop on Fleet and move all the workers to the traps on Cedar. He thought to himself the Fleet area was too hot, so he planned to direct all the traffic to Cedar from now on. His phone rang again. It was his big homie Gunner. "What's poppin?" New Bag asked as he answered the phone." "Rico got snatched by the Feds this morning. Close all the spots on Fleet for good." Gunner

said. "Damn, that's crazy, but I'm two steps ahead of you. I moved everybody over to Cedar, but what happened though?" New Bag asked. "S***, we think that white boy from the West Side is telling." Gunnar said. "I got a few drops on the West Side, and they told me dude had gotten snatched by the Feds a couple of weeks ago. I figured Rico knew because the streets knew. So do you think I should move the Stash House to another location, and what about them f****** dogs? If Rico ain't there, I can't get in. The dogs would tear my ass up. I got a key, but them dogs ain't nothing to play with," New Bag said.

"I will go over there this evening and take the dogs to my house. S***, I got to go grab the other two from Rico's main house since he is in CCA. I guess I got to take the dogs. They don't know anybody else, but yeah, move the stash house. Ain't no telling If the Feds are hip to that spot. The fuck I'm going to do with six big ass Rottweilers?" "Take them to the pound," New Bag said. "Rico would have a heart attack because he loves those dogs. What I'm supposed to do when it's time to reload s***?" New Bag asked. "I don't know right this moment, but we will figure out something. I'm definitely not coming back into play", Gunner said, "so I will set up a drop off spot and pick up spot. but since Rico is out the equation. You might have to put half the money up for the load by them not really knowing you personally, but I would definitely vouch for you because I know you are a thousand percent loyal and trustworthy. How many units left anyway? New Bag asked. "I'm still loaded, but I was asking so I'm prepared for what lies ahead. You taught me that big homie." New Bag said.

"Make sure you move the stash house tonight, and make sure the spot is not under surveillance. If you see anything fishy don't stop, keep it pushing," Gunner said. "Shidd, there are 190 units left. You know how much money that is?" New Bag said. "Yeah, I know how much money that is, but if the Feds are watching the spot, do you know how much time that is? Life, and life in the Feds mean until you die nigga." Gunner said. "I will call you later once I roll through there and take a look. If everything is good, I'm going to grab the dogs, and then you gotta move that s*** as soon as possible." After they ended the call, New Bag looked at his young boy riding with him and said "shidd ain't no way I'm leaving all them kilos. F*** tha Feds!" New Bag said.

Chapter 28

Back In Mexico.

HECTOR

Hector was pacing back and forth. He sent his men to retrieve the rest of the money from El'Rosso. Now he had a real tough decision to make - send the kids back in one piece or send them back piece by piece in the box. If he spared El'Rosso this time, he knew in his gut it would come back to haunt him. As he stood in the smelly room where the children were being held, his phone rang. "Boss, we've retrieved the money. Instead of it being 500 million, it's double that with a note," said one of Hector's workers. "What does the note say?" Hector asked. "It says *you won't live long enough to enjoy it, I know my children are going to be killed. I only paid the ransom so my wife will forgive me for putting my loved ones in harm's way. I will not rest until your head is sitting before me on a plate'.*" Hector told his men to return to the estate, and walked to the table where all types of knives and blades lay. He grabbed a large machete. He turned and walked up to the little girl first, and with a swift blow he decapitated her small head from her tiny body. It hit the floor with a dull thud. He then turned towards the boy, and swoosh, the machete removed the second child's head as well. He turned to his workers standing around and said "box both heads sitting on a plate, and mail them to El'Rosso with a note that says *dinner is served, and dessert is on the*

way. Thanks for the billion dollars my friend,
and I hope your wife will forgive you.

JULIO.

Julio was out at the farm. He was responsible
for getting the load ready for a shipment that
was about to be transported to the states. He's
only handling these things until Chi- Chi fully
recovers, which should be real soon. He's
been out of the hospital for four weeks now.
For somebody who took 15 bullets close range,
he's doing very well. Julio was wrapping things
up at the farm. He was needed at his boss
Hector's estate, so he spoke with a few other
farm workers and walked to his truck. The
driver had the back door open waiting for Julio
to climb in. Julio hated having a driver, but this
war with the Lamia Cartel gave him no choice.
It took longer to get to Hector's than usual, due
to them making sure they weren't being
followed. Julio was escorted into the main
foyer where he was greeted by Chi-Chi and
Hector. "How's it going, my good friend?" Chi-
Chi walked over to the bar to make three drinks
while his boss Hector began discussing their
next move. He figured they might as well go
full force at El'Rosso, and he planned to get rid
of this problem once and for all. A team of
trained killers will ambush him while he is
attending his children's funeral. Hector was
always taught to never kick someone when

they were down - kill them, and that's just what he planned to do. Julio asked "where do I come into play on this?", and Hector said "you will be in charge of the team that's going to carry out the hit. Chi Chi will fill you in on the details. We have no room for error."

Back in Miami…

HEAD HONCHO

Head Honcho was just leaving the hospital after visiting Pedro as he did every week. Now being the head of the Looney Squad Mob, his hands were full, and he felt like he was working for the enemy. He knew the Cash Money Chicks were the ones who took the hit that was put on Pedro. He was out on South Beach cruising, enjoying the breeze coming off the ocean and in deep thought when he spotted three sexy women. It couldn't be, he thought. He followed them with his eyes as they entered a food spot called Wet Willie's. He pulled his drop top Lambo up in front of the spot and got out. He entered and walked upstairs to the second level. When the triplets placed their orders, he walked up to the counter and added his order to theirs and told the clerk he would be paying the bill. He paid for their food and told the woman behind the counter to please have his food brought out front and that he would be seated at one of the tables enjoying this beautiful weather. He smiled at the triplets.

He had not been seated for even five minutes before Tiff approached him, carrying both of their foods. I thought the least I could do was bring your food out to you since you paid for me and my sisters' food too. By the way, "thank you," Tiff said. "It was my pleasure," he responded. "How rude of me. My name is Preston, and yours?" "My name is Tiff, and my sisters are Tee and Lee." "Wow, how lucky can one be! Not just one, but three sexy women," Head Honcho said smiling. Tiff began to blush and said "So you're out going for a stroll along Ocean Drive to enjoy the view ? "Something like that," he responded, "but I prefer to drive and pointed in the direction of the convertible Lambo that sat directly in front of Wet Willie's. When Tiff saw it, her pussy began to instantly become wet and her brain went into plot mode. She was possibly looking at her next victim! Everything about this man in front of her says *money*, a whole lot of money! He broke her out of her daze by saying "Hello, Earth to Tiff." She returned her gaze on him and said "excuse me," and started laughing softly. He had to find a way to find out if these three sexy ladies were, in fact, the Cash Money Chicks. He invited them to accompany him at a pool party that was being thrown by one of his close friends, an owner of high end restaurants all over Miami. He soon has his answer to the million-dollar question.

Chapter 29

Back In Cleveland.

Lenny still didn't believe Rico was at CCA, and to make matters worse they f****** placed him on the pod that Lenny was on. After the run-in with Rico in the cafeteria, he asked for a separation. He knew it was just a matter of time before Rico figured everything out. There were all kinds of death threats coming his way. The Feds ended up moving him to another location because they feared for his safety. The case was just getting started, and they wanted to keep their star witness in good shape. That's how the FBI does us. You are up and then you are thrown to the wolves. If you are not strong enough to fight them off, you become food. Lenny was definitely going to become food at the level he played the game. If you get popped, ain't no snitching. At least not without consequences. He walked into MMC and was processed and housed on a PC (Protective Custody) block. Every inmate on this pod had snitched on someone at one point or another. He started to feel like he should have never cooperated. He had a bad feeling that his days were numbered, and he just doesn't know how right he was.

400.

New Bag was able to get the remaining kilos out of the Stash House. He set up another stash spot on the West Side off of State Road. It was a nice quiet street. He actually bought the house three months earlier to put one of his little lady friends in, but they ended up not f****** around anymore. This house would be perfect. He had to get the floor customized so he could hide the product in the floor without it being detected. He also had a top-of-the-line alarm system installed with video cameras attached directly to his cell phone. He had a landscaping company come out every week to keep the lawn well maintained. To the naked eye, he blended right in when he came and went. He was still running through units left and right and was even serving drops that Rico had. He had his phones and Rico's phone, so he was constantly on the go - no chill time.

It was time he promoted one of his youngest who had become pretty good. At this rate he will burn himself out, so he called his young boy Tim. Tim was young, but Tim was a grinding motherfucker and never asked to be fronted. He grinded his way from five grams to buying 500 grams every trip and his money was always right, so New Bag was about to level him up. He met him at a bar called The Wolf Den. Tim pulled into the parking lot and got out. He walked over to New Bag's car and got in the passenger seat.

New Bag pulled off heading to the stash spot. When they walked in, unlike the Stash House that Rico and Gunnar had, this b**** was laid out with top-of-the-line everything. He turned to Tim and asked "are you ready to get some real money?" Tim answered, "I was born ready," and just like that, Tim was the second in charge. He went from buying 500 grams to selling n***** kilos all over Cleveland. New

Bag was proud of his protege. Shidd, he was running through more units than New Bag. He always knew Tim was destined to be a boss by the way he carried himself, the way he handled situations and the way he got to the bag. Only boss niggas move like that. Out of every hundred niggas only one is fit to be a boss. That's just how life goes and the other ninety nine are meant to be workers. Everybody has a role to play. New Bag's personal cell phone rang and it was Gunner. "What's up Big Homie?" New Bag said. "Shit, what's up?" he said. "Why you ain't been answering Rico's calls? He's been calling you for a few days now" he said. "No disrespect to big homie, but Rico thinks I'm still a little 400. Those days are over with, "New Bag said. "I'm running through the pack. His money is always on point, so why the f*** I got to answer my phone. I know what needs to be done and I don't need nobody telling me what to do. I know how to move." "I feel you Youngin," Gunner retorted, "but you still got to show respect to the hand that's feeding you. It's rules to this s***. Next time that Nigga call, answer your phone and don't take this the wrong way, but I'm not asking, I'm telling you answer your phone." Gunnar said then he hung up. New Bag felt where Gunner was coming from. He just didn't like to answer to Rico. Rico spoke to him as if he was still a little nigga, and it just didn't sit well, but next time Rico call he definitely would answer so he could let Rico know now he was the head nigga in charge.

Chapter 30

RICO.

Shit was looking all bad for Rico. *Lenny's hoe ass done put the Feds on him!* He was their star witness. He never in a million years would have seen this coming. He ran a smooth operation, so he thought, but he ain't trippin. This shit come with the game and he's a nigga getting to a real bag. There are people in a way higher position than him, but cooperating with the Feds is not an option, at least not for him. He calls his old head a few times and he calls Gunner only when it's important. He's got a stable of hoes, so he is always on the phone or getting a visit. The only thing that be getting him out his hookup is the young n**** 400 never answering his f****** phone, Rico thought to himself. *I hear he got n***** out there calling him New Bag little Nigga letting that paper chang him, I'm going to f*** around have to turn the faucet off on little homie, he acts as if I'm not the one supplying the water that quenches his thirst.* One of the rules of the game is never bite the hand that feeds you.

As Rico was coming off the floor from doing his push ups, he saw a crowd begin to form. There was a fight about to take place. Rico learned quickly the Feds is not like doing state time. All cities in Ohio stick together, and if one city gets into it with another state, then we all come together. There is power in numbers. This morning one of Rico's homies had some beef with a nigga from DC, so he was quick to approach. Both sides were ready to go, but neither side wanted to be on lockdown because of a riot, so luckily the situation was defused and everyone returned to what they were doing. There definitely would be a lot of tension throughout the prison for a while.

After finishing his workout routine, he headed to his cell. His cellie was whipping up a mean break. "S*** right on time," Rico said. "You already know," he replied. Rico's celly was a nigga from down the way named Face. Cool nigga - he used to run with Rico's older nigga, Bussy from Longwood, so they clicked right out the gate. Rico grabbed his s*** and went and jumped in the shower. After showering, he banged his nachos bowl that his celly had made, shook him up a foxy, which is coffee and Kool-Aid with hot water and ice cubes shaken up. Man, bitch tastes good. After shaking up his foxy, he headed to the phone to shoot his one tooth.

BIG MOBY

Mo Skrill was older, but he still liked to be in the mix. He used to have the Fleet area in a choke hold, but you know as time passed by the new generation started to come into play. They grind totally differently. They are reckless and wild, and fear no consequences. So, he stepped back and let the youngest takeover, but he still slid through to hit his drops, stopping at the barber shop between 59th and 60th and chopping it with Rog every now and then. For the most part, though, he was at the crib with his wife and kids. He also bought a house in Maple Heights. Like Trucker J, they wanted to give their kids a better environment and more opportunities than they had growing up.

Mo was just pulling in his driveway when his phone started going off. First thing he thought was he was not going back down on Fleet, but when he looked at the phone it was his personal phone ringing. He answered it and it was a collect call from his nephew Rico calling from CCA. He didn't even know Rico was locked up. He hadn't seen him around but he just figured he was staying out the way. He pushed one to accept the call. "What's up?" they both said at the same time. "Shidd, I can't call it another day another dollar." Rico said. "What the f*** you doing at CCA?" Mo asked. "Unc, Fed snatched me because I was f****** with the white boy from 73rd and Colgate. Hoe ass nigga ended up telling on me." "I told you all money ain't good money," Mo said. "I know," Rico said, "but I can't cry over spilled milk. I'm just waiting to see what they are gonna offer me. When it's all said and done this some light s*** . At the end they could be burying niggas in this b****. So what's been going on with you? How's the family? Rico asked. "You know, same old s***, busting my ass to take care of my household. Your auntie is driving me crazy like always and junior's getting bigger and starting to get into everything." Mo answered. "That's what's up!" Rico said. "Hey you know Montay down there?" Mo asked. "No, I thought he was at

CCA, but the Feds didn't move him yet. He's still in the County. Man he's crazy as a motherfuker. Who gets shot and then goes to the hospital with two guns on them? Nigga didn't get rid of them guns before his crazy ass went to the emergency," Rico said. "That ain't what happened," Mo said. "It's a long story, but are you good , do you need anything?" "Just make sure you put money on an account for me so I can call straight through," Rico said. There is one thing I might need you to do. My little n**** who I got running s*** is starting to let the money go to his head, so I'm going to cut off the faucet on him. If I need you to step in to run Point, can I depend on you to make the basket Rico said, n**** who taught you how to get to the bag did you forget, my fault but I got to go is count time Rico said as he hung up the phone,

Moby was in deep thought when his wife came out the back door and said to him, "I need to run to the store. "Who was you sitting out here talkin to you on the phone?" Kim asked. He just looked at her and gave her the car keys and turned to go into the house. She was right on his heels. "So you don't hear me? You was just hearing whatever b**** that was on the phone!" Moby turned around and said "if your nephew is a bitch, then I guess I was on the phone with a bitch! He walked away and left her standing there feeling and looking stupid as f***.

Chapter 31

EL ROSSO.

El'Rosso and his wife are pulling up to the front of the large church. His wife has been going crazy ever since packages were delivered to their home. When she got the packages inside and opened them, she fainted. Her husband walked towards the boxes, already knowing what was inside. The boxes contained the heads of his beloved children. He showed no emotion. He knew he would never see his kids alive again before this day. This is the world that we live in. His driver opened the back door of the limousine. He and his wife stepped out. She was holding on to his arm as if she was a child. She couldn't believe that just past the church doors lay her babies inside closed caskets. Both front doors opened at the same time by the doorkeepers. El'Rosso and his wife were led inside. The church was packed with family members only. El'Rosso wasn't taking any chances. It was a long and painful service. There was a photo of each child on top of the pink casket and the blue casket. Their mother broke down at least a dozen times. Who can blame her? No one knows what it's like to bury a child unless they have lost a child themselves. After the service they were en route to the burial site.

As they pulled through the gates of the cemetery, El'Rosso noticed there were quite a few people around the gravesite, but what stood out was not one was holding flowers or balloons. They were all males in all black. Just as El'Rosso told his driver not to stop, bullets came from every direction. All he could do was pray the bulletproof car could withstand the impact from the gunfire. Once the trained shooters realized they f***** up the hit by not waiting for El'Rosso to exit his vehicle, they were now in a full-blown shootout with El Rosso's gunmen. El'Rosso watched it all unfold right before his eyes, safely inside his car. All of a sudden, the car in front of the car he was riding in exploded. He told his driver to go. He knew his car was bulletproof, but he knew it could not withstand a round from the grenade launcher that was now being fired by one of the attackers. The driver floored it. There were dead bodies everywhere as his car roared up the narrow path that ran through the cemetery. Bullets were still hitting the vehicle. If he had stepped one foot out of that limousine, he would have been gunned down instantly. All he thought about as he was being driven away to safety was revenge. He had underestimated Hector and it cost him dearly. He would never rest until he settled the score.

JULIO.

Julio just received information that the hit on El'Rosso did not go as planned. He was furious. How could a well put together plan fail? He didn't want to deliver the bad news to his boss, but he had no choice. After he learned all the details, he made the drive to Hector's Estate. As he approached the gate, he noticed more guards than usual. He figured the news had already reached his boss. He exited the vehicle and entered the mansion where he was led to Hector and Chi-Chi, who were talking to several heavily armed gunmen. Hector's face told it all. He turned towards Julio and told him "You're going back to the States, Chi-Chi is fully recovered, and there are some things you need to address right away with a few of our friends back in the States. Julio didn't respond. He knew better, especially when Hector was in this state of mind. Julio called ahead and told them to get the jet ready. Two hours later he was up in the air on his way back to the States. To tell the truth, he was glad he was being sent back. He hated being in Mexico. All he thought about the whole time was Miami, the scenery and the weather. He still had to wait for Chi-Chi to send the details, but until then he will be enjoying the great weather. He lay back in his captain chair on the jet and fell asleep.

CHI-CHI.

Chi-Chi was back mobile and it felt good to get out for some fresh air, but he would never make the same mistake twice. He kept armed guards with him everywhere he went. He was in route to oversee the product being processed for the next shipment. That was the reason Julio was sent back to the States so he could meet the new buyer. Hector had just set up a huge deal with the African, but they lived in the States now. They had a pipeline coming from their homeland, but due to the CIA, it was shut down. Chi-Chi had just gotten off the phone with Hector giving him the details.

Julio was scheduled to have a meet and greet with the African so he could give him the details on how the load would be dropped and a location for a pick up for the payment could be put in place. They were both new to each other, so trust was something that would have to be earned on both sides of the fence, especially dealing with that amount of money. After ending his call with Julio, he called Hector and informed his boss that everything was lined up and we're good to go, he had a long night ahead of him at the Farm, once the shipment is ready to roll, he will head to his estate that's just as elegant as Hector's, once he's in route, he will give Trucker J. a call to give him a heads up on the upcoming run.

Chapter 32

Back In Miami

TINY.

Tiny was overseeing the bar at the club house tonight. Margelia was still in Cleveland attending a meeting for the Lit Life MCS. The bar was jumping, and it became one of the places to be on the weekend and not just for Bikers, but for anyone who was really trying to step out and have a good time. Yeah, you had you a few episodes when a patron got too drunk and started dumb s***, but for the most part it was drama free. This was mainly because if you caused any problems inside the clubhouse, then Lit Life would lock the doors and literally, ain't no telling what they would do to you. Tiny was headed to the office to start tallying up the night's count. On Friday, Saturday and Sunday they raked in that bag. They might be an MC, but the set up to their establishment is upscale, and all are welcome. On Wednesdays it is mostly filled with Haitians. They called it Little Haiti Wednesday Other days it's just like any other club or bar. It is always open to the public and it is always going. Shidd, we in Miami!

Tiny was chilling in the office talking on the phone and watching the cameras. He spotted one of the triplets walking up to the bar. She had on a see-through shirt and matching skirt. Some sexy ass heels just added to her already banging ass figure, and long ass silky hair (which was all hers). She placed an order. The bartender returned with her Long Island and a glass of water with lemons in it. She paid for her drink and walked towards a booth. Tiny loved the way she sucked dick and she a good f***. Once she did a few lines she would fuck a nigga to his grave and still want some more. There is something about a female on coke. It increases your sex drive to overdrive.

Tiny walked out of the office and went to where Tee was sitting. As soon as she saw him she looked away smiling. Just as bad, Tiny wanted her; she wanted him. It was a win-win for her. She was getting some good-ass dick and the best cocaine in Miami at the same time. "What's up my little bust it baby?" Tiny said as he approached. She looked at him with that look in her eyes. Right then Tiny knew that they were on the same page. "Nothing . . . just came out for drinks," she said. "Where are your sisters," he asked, "I didn't see them come in with you." "They are out doing them. Lee is somewhere getting her pussy eaten and Tiff is with her new male friend. We bumped into him a few weeks ago at Wet Willies, and he has been hounding her ever since. You know her, she plans on sucking him to death." They both laughed, because when Tiff got done with dude, he would be flat broke and most likely found dead. "So, what's the move for the night?" Tee asked. "It's still early. As soon as it starts to slow down, I'm going to do my count on what the nights take is and then we can head to the party room." Tiny said. "Count me all the way in," she said and took a big gulp of her Long Island.

CASH MONEY CHICKS.

Tee went into the ladies room, hoping like hell it was empty. Tiny had given her an eight ball of coke to get her going. He loved when she was in a party mode, because she was much more aggressive. She would be riding his dick, just jump up to do a line, then bend over and say, "eat this ass, then stick your dick in it and fuck this ass now!" That is why he loved hooking up with her. She was open to try anything, and I mean anything! There were a few people inside the restroom. She went into one of the stalls, sat on the toilet and opened the bag of coke.   She rolled up a twenty dollar bill and before she sniffed a couple of lines, she put the bag up to her nose. She loved the smell of coke. If you did coke, it was one of the best smells in the world. It automatically made your pussy wet or your dick hard. She stuck her finger in the bag and rubbed some around on her gums. She snorted one line up one nostril and it hit her brain instantly. She felt like she was cumming on herself. She did another line up the other nostril, and BAM, she wanted to f*** right now. She was so high and horny she opened her legs and began to play with her pussy right there. She couldn't help it. She was so into it, she didn't realize she was moaning out loud. The few ladies outside of her stall that were in the restroom fixing their hair or washing their hands were like *okay???*

Hearing the moaning, they all exited the bathroom except for one female. She was turned on. Her pussy was wet and throbbing. She tapped on the stall door and said can I join you? Tee was caught off guard, but she was so high and on her fourth nut, she kicked the stall door open as she sat on the toilet with her legs spread wide open and her cum juices everywhere. All the lady saw was a fat pretty pussy with a clitoris so big you couldn't help but want to suck it, and that's just what she did.

She got down between her thighs and went to town sticking her finger in her pussy while she licked it. Tee was f****** her face rough, and the woman loved it. They went on sucking each other for an hour. So many ladies had come in and gone out of the restroom and couldn't believe it. Some were even turned on themselves. When Tee and the woman finally had enough, they did a few lines, and Tee invited her to the party room tonight with herself and Tiny. She wanted some more of that pussy.

TIFF.

Tiff was at the mall spending money with her new male friend, Preston also known as Head Honcho. She spent a few nights with him at one of his beach houses, but she didn't notice a safe anywhere. She was trying to gain his trust and it seemed he felt comfortable showing her where his mansion was located. The night he invited them to the pool party they hit it off, and he didn't try to have sex with her. He did mention something about the group of sexy ladies that called themselves Cash Money Chicks. Tiff blew it off. She didn't understand where it came from, but she was definitely going to find out. She noticed Preston had no problem spending money, but she still didn't know how he made his money.

After dining at a fabulous restaurant they were en route to yet another one of Preston's friend's parties. Tiff had on an all-white Gucci dress with some silver red bottoms and a silver clutch bag. Of course, her jewelry was on point. Preston was Dapper in his all- white Armani suit. He wore a pair of Hermans with a matching belt. On his wrist rested a presidential Rolex. Now this party was nothing like the pool party. At the pool party everyone was getting drunk, and when I say drunk, I'm talking white girl wasted. This event was far more upscale. Everyone in Miami knows upscale parties mean platters of free cocaine. Every inch of the backyard and the house were full of guests enjoying themselves. Waiters were walking around refilling glass after glass. Tiff walked around eating, drinking and dancing until her feet were killing her. She walked up to the table where the platter of coke was located. She bent over and in a flash, she had done two lines. Her whole body relaxed. When she returned to their table she saw Preston standing a few feet away talking to someone that looked kind of familiar. She just couldn't put a finger on it. He smiled and waved her over. As she approached, it hit her that he was the driver of the limousine the night they hit Pedro. She prayed he didn't remember her. Preston introduced her as his lady friend, Tiff, and I extended my hand in a greeting gesture and said nice to meet you. He stared for a second too long then he finally spoke, "nice to meet you as well."

HEAD HONCHO.

Head Honcho had a good feeling that the sisters were the ones responsible for his dad Pedro laying in a coma this very moment. He brought up the Cash Money Chick's name, but she changed the subject and he left it alone. He didn't want to push it, but that was his reason for calling her over tonight at the party. when he was talking to the man who was driving his father the night he was shot. The driver couldn't say for sure if he remembered her, but he thought she looked familiar.

As he pulled up to the upscale condo, they were both in deep thought. She felt something wasn't quite right. They pulled into the underground parking area and he sensed she was a little distant. As soon as he put the car in park, he grabbed her by her long silky hair and kissed her long and hard. It was more passionate than he wanted it to be, but he got caught up in the moment and her beauty, everything about her was beautiful, her face, her frame, her feet. He was so caught up, he forgot she could possibly be the enemy. They exited the car, both in deep thought, but both knew tonight they definitely wanted each other. As they got off the elevator, a man was staring at Tiff as if he knew her. Tiff didn't notice, but Preston did, so he took a mental note to ask the guy who was getting on the elevator if he knew her previously. Once inside, they wasted no time going at each other like wild animals in heat.

Chapter 33

Back to Cleveland

TRUCKER J.

I had just received a text from Chi-Chi about a pick-up and drop that was scheduled for the following week. That meant I needed to get on the road as soon as possible. Just like always, of course, Toya wasn't too happy about me being called back to work so soon. I told her that I didn't have a run coming up for a few weeks. I was trying to pack my over-the-road bag, and also let her know that I promised not to be gone long. I hate when she gives me that sad look with her bottom lip out. Being on the road and away from Toya and the twins got me thinking about hiring a driver that could drive for me. I thought seriously about buying and putting four more trucks on the road. That way, I would still make a nice amount of cash flow, but I would free up all my time. I would just run my trucking company from my home office. I would need to buy or lease a place to park my rigs. After packing, I prepared a big breakfast for Ms. LB and the twins. We had breakfast and afterwards, she bathed the boys.

I was on the phone touching base with Chi-Chi. Once I ended the call, I walked into the bathroom and turned the shower on and stripped down. Stepping in, I let the water run over my body. I felt a pair of hands rubbing my back. It was Toya. I smiled. She said "I love you." I turned to face her and said "I love you more." We started kissing. I asked what the boys were doing. She said, "they're watching cartoons and eating grapes." I pulled her close to me and lifted her just enough to slide my rock-hard dick into her soaking wet pussy. We made love, then we bathed each other. Once we were dried off and putting our clothes on, I turned to Toya and said "I'll have a surprise for you when I get back, and I think you're going to love it." She said "I hope it's some more of that dick I can't get enough of." We both started laughing, then she said "I'm dead serious." I said "I know, that's why I was laughing, but I gotta get going. I will call you as soon as I get settled in the truck, okay?" I gave her a kiss then went to tell my boys I would see them later and to be good for their mommy. I grabbed my over-the-road back and headed out the door.

Days Later.

I was halfway to the pickup location. The traffic had been crazy, but now I'm rolling. I love when the road is open and flowing. My phone started ringing. The only person it could be was Toya. *Oh, she was FaceTiming me.* "Hey Ms. LB!" She started laughing. "How's it going?" she asked. I said "It's going baby. How are you and the boys, and where are y'all at? It looks like you are in the pet store." "We are," she answered. "They wanted a turtle, so I am here buying a turtle. I said "Well you know you will have to buy two so they don't be fussing." "I know," Toya said. "but I just wanted to say love you and drive safe." "Love you more," I said before she hung up. Things like that make me feel whole and complete. A few days later, I was entertaining Las Cruces, New Mexico. I was a couple hours away from my pick-up location.

WHITE BOY LENNY.

Lenny went before a grand jury. There was no turning back now. His new name was Snitch Lenny, and it was all through the streets and jails. Some couldn't believe that crazy ass Lenny telling. Shidd, the Feds got a way to make the most gangster nigga tell. Niggas would tell on their own mama when facing football numbers. Lenny was coming back from court, and he was pissed. He just found out even after cooperating and giving up Rico, he still had to do time. He thought he would be released and relocated somewhere in the witness protection program. "Only in the movies," he said. It finally hit him that the Feds played him, and now he was a dead man walking.

Twenty years was his least concern, how could he make it through two years, let alone twenty being labeled a snitch. *Damn* was all he could say. He lay in his cell night after night wishing he would die in his sleep and escape this nightmare. He always woke up to be smacked in the face by reality and also smacked by his new cellmate. A huge black guy they called Bonecrusher. Yeah, he had also snitched on someone. The reason he didn't like Lenny was because Lenny was white. For the past two weeks since being moved, his new cellie had been physically abusing him. Today would be his last. As soon as he woke Lenny up with a slap to the face, Lenny sprung from his bed like a frightened cat. The only thing different about today was in his left hand he held a shank made out of a ruler he stole out of the school area, with quick blows he began stabbing Bonecrusher in the neck and stomach. He must have blanked out because he stabbed him over 40 times. Another inmate heard his screams and called for the CO's. He is killing him.

The unit was shut down and the riot squad came in full force. Too bad it was too late for

Bonecrusher. He was dead long before they made it to their cell. Lenny was pepper sprayed and tackled to the floor. There was blood everywhere. He was cuffed and dragged to the Special Housing Unit (SHU) The SHU is a disciplinary unit for housing inmates that have violated one of the prison rules in one form or another. He would most likely be in the SHU throughout his Court proceedings. Once he is sentenced, he would be transferred to his parent institution where he would still have to do like twelve months in the shu before being house on a unit in General population, Lenny just turned his twenty year sentence into a life sentence for killing his cellmate, but he didn't give a fuck. Twenty years is life to him, and he still has to worry about Rico putting money on his head. No matter where he goes he will have to sleep with one eye open, and always be on full alert, Lenny felt like he dug his own grave and jumped head first into it.

MARGIELA.

Margelia was chilling with a few of his special people at the Swerve Grill, one of his favorite spots in Cleveland. While they were eating, a young dude walked in wearing so much jewelry you would have thought he was a rapper. He approached the table and spoke to one of the guys that Margelia was meeting with. He was respectful and then he excused himself.

Margelia liked the way he carried himself and took a mental note. He plans to reach out to him at a later date. After Margelia pulled out of the Swerve, he slid through the 10th Ward and bumped into a few of his close partners. They chopped it up for a minute and updated him on the City's latest demos. Ain't too much changed - same game, just new players out on the playing field. One of his partners was telling him how this new young dude from somewhere around the Cedar area was doing big numbers and that he had that s*** you could do backflips on. They told him he ran under niggas from the Fleet named Gunner and Rico, but Gunner was done with the streets. They told him that he had opened up restaurants and a club, upscale joints too. They are nice as f*** on the inside. The streets say he walked away from the game with a few million. Rumor is Rico's old head is plugged in with the cartel, shit comes straight from Mexico.

"So, what's up with Rico?" Margelia's partner asked. "The nigga got snatched up by the ABC boys a couple months ago. Now the young boy I was just telling you about is the running point. The nigga got everybody calling him New Bag." Margelia had just heard that name today. He was trying to link it with a face, then he remembered the young boy at the Swerve had introduced himself as New Bag. So young n**** getting to the bag like that,? Margelia asked. Getting to it is an understatement. There are some heavy hitters in the City, but he's in the top five and his squad is nothing to play with. Youngin came from the trenches - robbery, home invasion, quick to put shit down, so he only f*** with the slums, and they are trained to go at the drop of a dime. Margelia dapped his nigga and said he had a couple other people he needed to see. He headed out Solon to meet up with a chick he had running his salons. You would never know. The city thinks she's the owner, and that's just how he liked it. If you were just a bypasser, it looks as if the couple were packing to go on vacation, but really Margelia was transferring duffle bags of kilos to her trunk. She didn't only run his salons, she also held anywhere from 100 to 200 hundred kilos at a time for him. Her brother is in charge of getting the product out on the streets and holding the money in safe locations. Margelia always stressed to never have all the money in one place. You never know. It is better to be safe than sorry. Margelia was headed to The 9 downtown where he had a room. No, he was not alone. His lovely wife to be one day was waiting at the suite just chilling. It has been a long day. She couldn't wait for Margelia to get back.

Chapter 34

NEW BAG.

New Bag had shit poppin. He was running through units like a prostitute. He was getting low and didn't have a clue on who he could f*** with, that could fill his order and have Grade A product. Since the fallout with Rico the other day when he called, bitch told him he was cut off, so he got to find a plug and he got to do it quickly. My one n**** said he got a cousin from across town that he be supplying the 10th Ward and a few other parts of Cleveland. He moved out to Miami, but would be in the city for a couple of days. "Shidd, make it happen!" New Bag told him. He jumped on his cell phone and called. After a few minutes talking to his people, he ended the call and said "we are good for the night. He wants us to meet him at the Rise located in Severance."

Later that night, New Bag and five of his youngest walked into the Rise looking like Big Meech BMF is Free. So much ice on, you would have thought somebody cut the lights on. This was supposed to be a meet and greet, but dude came from nothing and he knew the first impression was everything. Sometimes in life you only get that one chance and he refused to f*** this up. Before you knew it, he had his section overflowing with bottles. To take it over the top, the DJ announced that New Bag bought the bar out. Drinks are free for everybody for the rest of the night. The Club went crazy.

Margelia was seated off to the left of the bar. New Bag's homie gave him the signal to let him know it was time. As he walked towards Margelia, his gut told him it was on and popping. He approached, stuck his hand out and introduced himself. Margelia told him to take a seat. After the meeting it was written in stone. New Bag had just locked in a new plug, and he was getting a cheaper price. Margelia was a good judge of character, so he knew this young n**** was a paper chaser to the heart. New Bag will receive his first shipment in six days - a hundred kilos you can put a two on it at sixty a unit. Margelia wanted half the money up front until he became comfortable with New Bag, which was not an issue soon. As soon as the meet and greet was over, New Bag bounced. Mission accomplished. Back to the swamps he goes.

GUNNER.

Gunner walked out of the kitchen after making sure everything was good for the night. His first club took off so fast, he had to open another and ride the highway wave while the tide was in full force. Rico called him earlier and told him 400 D'Nelle aka New Bag was cut off, but he saw this coming. There was too much tension between the two of them. He was out of the game, but Rico was his right-hand. He asked Rico what he was going to do next. Rico told him the move with the new point guard. Gunner couldn't help but laugh. This nigga locked up and still at the playboard drawing up plays. While he was going over the details for the night's event, New Bag walked through the front door. "What's up Big Homie? Shit going to be crazy tonight. The City is saying you are bringing Money Man and Money Bagg out to perform. Damn, you got the juice. Two heavy hitters at the same damn time. I see you getting your grown man on doing your business thang. I respect it. Only thing better than a bag is a *new bag*." They both laughed.

"I see you still getting to a new bag," said Gunner. "Ain't no other way. I heard you and Rico fell out. What's that about?" Gunner asked. "You already know, he wanted to control me," New Bag replied. "Nigga crazy as f***, so he tried to hold the plug over my head like I'm going to turn the faucet off, so I said nigga that shit only work when you're dealing with a thirsty nigga. F*** you and your plug, and I banged on the nigga." Gunner asked, "So now what are you going to do? You know I'm out and I'm not coming back into play." "I would never ask you to come back," New Bag said, "you made it out. I hope when it's my time to exit the game that I'm as smart as you were, but I already knocked a plug - the one dude from across town that runs the MC. He is the leader of the Lit Life MC." "Are you talking about Margelia?" Gunner asked. "He moved to Miami. Rumor is he being supplied by the cartel." "Yeah, that's dude," New Bag said. "I'm gonna run me up a new bag, put my youngins in position and I'm gonna fall all the way back. Shidd, I might even open up Some Clubs, have the city calling me Club New Bag." They both started laughing. "Well I'm glad everything worked out for you. Remember, make the money and don't let it make you," Gunner said. "Always, Big Homie," New Bag agreed. " . . . and I'm definitely going to be in the building tonight. VIP that is. Any other way will be uncivilized." Gunner said.

Back In Miami.

JULIO.

Julio was sitting in his diner waiting for Zenru the African to arrive. He was sipping coffee and reading the paper, his daily routine. He watched an all-white SUV pull up in front of the diner. A man exited the passenger door, and opened the back passenger door for a middle aged built man the color of tar to exit. They approached the front door of the diner and he stepped inside. I waved them over. He walked toward my table and took a seat. His men were on point. One posted right behind Zenrus chair, another inside the diner at the entryway, one outside the diner at the entranceway and one stood at the SUV rear door. I see Zenru covers all of his bases. We began with small talk and by the end of our meeting, both parties were feeling very pleased and eager to do business with one another. A drop point was put into play and a pickup location was also factored into play.

Before ending the meeting, Zenru said "to show my good faith, I would like to pay for this shipment up front." He snapped his fingers and his men went out to the SUV and returned with 10 large duffle bags, each holding 20 million, totaling out to 200 million. "Let this be the first step to us building a solid trusting Foundation," Zenru said. He and Julio shook hands, and Julio said "trust and loyalty, my good friend." After Julio's men put the duffel bags inside the walk-in freezer, he headed to his office. When his phone rang, it was Haitian Black. "What's going on, my good friend? Just calling to let you know the load is in," he said. "Okay, get it ready for transport to the drop spot. Let me know when it's on the move. They are already expecting it, so everything is in place." Julio said.

HEAD HONCHO.

Head Honcho is at one of their money spots. All you heard were money counters. It is a spacious condo with bags of money everywhere. Even though Lit Life MC took over Miami, Honcho still rakes in millions. He stands around talking on his phone to Tiff. He can't put his finger on it, but his gut is telling him she's bad news. He still hasn't had a talk with his neighbor to see if he knew Tiff from somewhere. After he handled what he had to at the money spot, Head Honcho put a call into Margiela so he could reload. He hated copping from the enemy, but for now this was the only way. He knew it was just a matter of time before his Pops would come out of that f****** coma he was in. Margelia answered, "What's up, Mr. Head Honcho?" trying to be funny, "you know what's up," Head Honcho replied." "I need to reload, okay? "I'm in Cleveland right now, but I will be back in Miami in a few days, or I can send Tiny your way." Margelia said. "No, I can wait till you get back. You know me and Tiny don't jug," Head Honcho said." "Alright, I'll hit your line soon as the plane lands." Margelia assured him. Honcho wanted to stick a pistol in Margelia's ass and blow his guts out literally. He called Tiff to make sure they were still on for tonight.

CASH MONEY CHICKS .

Tiff was just getting out of the shower when she heard her phone ringing. She rushed to answer. It was Preston. "Hey Bae," she said into the phone; pussy instantly getting moist thinking about all the nasty things he did to her, like sticking his tongue all the way in her ass, snorting coke off her clitorus then face f****** her pussy and ass for hours. She continued to dress after she confirmed that their date was still a go. She had been kicking it with Preston for a few months now, and she still didn't have a clue where he kept his money stashed. He always has a couple hundred thousand somewhere reachable.

Tee and Lee had left heading to the Lit Life Clubhouse. For the past week, Tee had been going every day of the week. It damn sure wasn't for the drinks. Once Tiff was dressed, she headed to meet this one chick who was supposed to introduce her to the rapper Rick Ross. Tiff had hopes that she would be able to get in with him and do what she does best. They met at these buildings in a rough part of Liv City. After she got the information she needed, she was on her way to meet Preston. Tonight she was going to rock his world. Once she put it down tonight she will know where he keeps every dollar he makes, trust and believe. She called her sisters and told them to be on standby, and don't f*** this up. This might be their only chance.

Chapter 35

CASH MONEY CHICKS.

Tee and Lee pulled up to the location Tiff had texted to their phones. Their job was to attach a tracking device on Preston's Lambo. That's it, once he dropped Tiff off and headed to his estate or any other location, they would be able to stake out and figure which ones held the cash. The triplets were not into moving drugs, so if they did happen to come across a stash house that held the product, they would pass the info along to one of their close friends back in Cleveland that lived to hit these types of licks. In return, the triplets would be paid for the information. Once they made sure the device was properly attached to the vehicle, Lee slid back into the car with Tee and shot Tiff a text that read *Good2Go*.

They pulled off and headed back to the Lit Life Clubhouse. Damn, it was packed! When they returned, every seat in the building was taken and people were wall to wall on the dance floor. They were headed to the bar when a bouncer approached them and said "Tiny got a booth reserved for y'all, and someone is up there to take you ladies' orders." They followed the bouncer as he led them through the crowd towards the VIP stairs. Once they were seated in their booth, a woman walked up and asked "can I take you lovely ladies' orders?" "Yes, I'd like a Long Island and a Moscato," Lee said. "and what will your friend be having the she asked, "I will be having a Sex on the Beach, light ice and a Moscato as well." The waiter went back to the bar to get their drinks. Tiny came into VIP smiling from ear-to-ear. "So how are the two most beautiful ladies in the world doing tonight?" he asked. "Since you had us a booth ready, we are doing a whole lot better," Tee said. "Well you know that y'all money is no good here, everything's on the house." Tiny said. "Thanks Tiny you're the best" Tee said, and winked at him with a devilish grin. As he was turning to walk away he turned and said "if y'all need anything, just let the waiters know and they will take care of you. When their drinks were on the table in front of them, they began to turn up.

EL ROSSO, JR.

Hassan hadn't heard from his father in over three years, but El'Rosso still made sure his illegitimate son had the best life could offer. He had enough money in his bank accounts to last a lifetime, maybe two. Hassan grew up in California. His mother was an average working-class woman. One summer while visiting some friends in Italy and dining at a famous restaurant, she was approached by a very attractive man. He stood five eleven, had jet black hair and sun-kissed skin. Once he spoke, she knew he was from Mexico or somewhere near that part of the region. They hit it off immediately. At the time, Hassan's mother did not know what El Rosso's occupation was. She just knew he dressed in expensive suits, traveled a lot, and was never alone. That made her think he was someone very important. He always had a driver and several armed guards. Once she became pregnant, he tried to convince her to get rid of the baby, but she refused, so he broke it off and never dealt with her again. He did make sure that she and her baby wanted for nothing. Not until many years later did he lay eyes on his son, and he knew one day he would eventually have to pull him into the fold and teach him how to stand at the head of a cartel. That day was finally here.

Hassan was looking at his phone as it was ringing. He couldn't believe his father was calling. He didn't know if he should be angry or happy, but he finally answered. "My son, how's it going?" El'Rosso asked. All Hassan could do was breathe into the phone. "Hello, are you still there?" "Yeah," El'Rosso, Jr. replied. "I'm here, just kind of shocked that you called." "Well," his father began, "it's time for you to learn how you were able to live the lifestyle of the rich and famous without ever working a day in your life. I know you're rich, you own a multi-million dollar company, no my son I'm afraid that's not the answer. I will send a car for you. Be ready. It's time you take your seat at the table." "What table are you talking about?" El'Rosso, Jr. asked. "You will see soon enough. A private jet will bring you to Mexico" his father replied. "Did you just say Mexico?"

he asked, "They're having a turf War as we speak in Mexico right now. There ain't no f****** way I'm going to Mexico." El'Rosso, Jr. retorted. "My son, I will explain everything to you once you arrive." "And why should I come to Mexico?" "Because your future depends on it."

Back in Cleveland.

NEW BAG.

New Bag was at his stash house running the bills through the money counter. He had to make sure the count was right. He was scheduled to meet Margelia at some place across town. He had to put half a million up front on this first load. Margelia was just feeling him out so he figured. He wasn't crying about it though. He was about to receive 100 units. It can take a two and that will give him 300 units of some flame. Yeah, numbers don't lie - three million when he's done, which is a two million dollar profit. Only thing better than the bag is a new bag, but y'all don't hear me though.

Margelia hit his phone just as he was putting the last of the money into the duffel bag. "What up Big Homie? You know where you are coming to, right? It's right off the freeway on 156th and Lakeshore," Margelia said.

"Yeah, I put the address into my GPS." New Bag answered. "I'm headed your way now." He walked outside, made sure the alarm was set then put the bags in the bed of the Dodge Ram pickup rental he was driving and made sure the bed cover was locked. Shidd, there is a half ticket back there! He jumped into the driver's seat and headed toward the freeway. He was listening to that new Moneybagg. Nigga be hollering and b**** know how to put it on. He pulled up to the address that was programmed in his GPS. Once he saw Margelia step onto the porch, he backed the truck up to the garage as he was instructed to do in the text message he had received. He got out and retrieved the duffel bag from the bed of the truck and walked to the back door. A chubby light skinned dude stood off to the side holding the door open for him to enter.

When he stepped into the door he was directly in the kitchen. Margelia stood in the doorway of the dining-room. About 14 members of Lite life were also there. New Bag handed the bags to one of Margelia's dudes. He asked "everything everything?" New Bag replied, "On the head. Counted twice myself Big Homie." Margelia said "This load is that and always will be. That you can put a four on and it's still going to be gunsmoke, guaranteed Youngin. New Bag started crunching the numbers. *Damn, a three million dollar profit when I'm done*, he thought to himself. *Where have you been all my life!* Margelia said "Your shit is in the bed of your truck. Hit me when you're done, I'm going to double you up next time. I needed a hungry young nigga like you. Like they say, one hand washes the other, and they both wash the face. The only thing better than a bag is a new bag."

MARGIELA.

Margelia put it on his newest member of the team. He knew the young New Bag had the potential and drive to take over the whole city with the right Source backing him up, and Margelia planned to be that source. Yeah, he had a few guys moving in the City, but he knew that New Bag was the one. He saw the same fire in his eyes that he once had in his when he was his age. He and his lady were en route to the airport. He didn't travel by private jet, but best believe, he was in first class whenever he flew. Before they jumped on the freeway, Margelia pulled up to Kim's on St. Clair for the wings his lady had ordered. Whenever they were in the City they made sure to stop at Kim's. They were smashing their food while waiting to board the plane. After they were called and seated comfortably on the plane with their feet up and waiting for takeoff, they engaged in small talk about life.

Margelia was in love with the mother of his daughter. Ever since middle school, having her in his life makes him feel whole. Every man whether he is in the streets or working a nine to five wants a woman he can come home to every night. She was his peace of mind and he was hers. Before they knew it, they were up in the air, and would be back in Miami in just a few hours. They both dozed off. When they opened their eyes, they were in Miami. All the passengers were being escorted off the plane. As soon as they hit the terminal, he called Head Honcho. The phone rang three times before he answered. "What's going on, King of Miami?" New Bag said, "As long as you know it, but anyway, I'm back." "What's the demo? Are you still grabbing 200 or are you ready to step it up?" Honcho asked. "Just my regular, and I feel that's a great number with your man Tiny setting up spots in all my areas," Head Honcho said. "I will text you the pickup location. You know the deal, one person to drive it back. Anything other than what we worked out is unacceptable."

After Margelia ended the call with Honcho, he called to the club house and told a few workers to get two hundred units ready for transport, he will be there in a few hours. how is everything going and where is Tiny he should be in the office yesterday counting take the person on the other end of the phone said, a vehicle was waiting out front for me and my lady at one of the many pick up areas at the airport, it was a quiet ride home she laid up against me listen to my heartbeat, and fell asleep once we arrive

I nudge her like baby were home she woke up I told her to go ahead and get comfortable I will grab the bags, and order us something to eat what do you have a taste for, she said steak, shrimp and loaded potatoes, thanks baby I gave her a kiss before I went to retrieve our luggage from the back of the truck.

Back In Miami.

A Few Hours Later.

I was at the club house in the back of the shop waiting as the last of the 200 units was being loaded into the van. When they were done, I had my dude Wink drive the van and follow me. I pulled up to the drop spot. Once I knew everything was cool and safe to make a trade-off, I called Head Honcho and told him the drop location and that he would have forty minutes to get to it. He pulled up and I gave him the keys to the van. He grabbed four duffle bags from the rear of the Suburban. Wink grabbed them and put them in the back of the truck. Honcho and I spoke briefly, then I pulled off.

HEAD HONCHO.

Honcho pulled off after picking up a load from Margiela. He was now en route to the garage he owned and runs as if it's a tire shop. The van was following behind him and was being driven by one of his loyal workers. He had just spent two million, and it was killing him that he couldn't get up the courage to put a bullet in Margelia's skull, the person behind his father now laying in the coma. In due time, however, Margellia and the Cash Money Chicks would pay. As he was pulling around the back, he noticed a vehicle with a dark tent parked a building over, but the thing was, he owns that building as well and it's vacant at the moment. It is strange that a car would be parked there. After the van was safely inside the garage, he told one of the workers to go check the car that was parked a lot over. As soon as the worker approached the vehicle it pulled off. He knew something fishy was going on, but he brushed it off. The worker returned and told Margelia the car pulled off before he could get up on it. "Why you didn't shoot the motherfucker up?" Margelia asked. The worker replied "What if it was the Feds?" "Then they would have been some dead Feds!" Margelia snapped. "Get this product put away and then drop this van off at the drop. I will call you sometime tomorrow so this s*** can be cut and put on the streets." Honcho jumped into his Hummer and backed out of the garage.

He was headed to the hospital to visit his old man. The doctor that attends to his pops left a message for him to call or stop by right away. In route to the hospital he called Tiff. She answered right away sounding happy. "Hey you," she said into the phone. "What do you have planned today?" Preston asked, "Hopefully you on a platter with a side of strawberries, and a bowl of hot chocolate, and a bottle of wine," she said. "We can definitely make that happen," Preston said. "As soon as I'm done handling a couple of things, I will give you a call and swing by and grab you." He was pulling into the parking lot. He went over to touch base with his neighbor at his condo. He had to find out for sure if Tiff and her sisters were, in fact, the Cash Money Chicks.

He walked to the entrance and headed straight for the stairs. He hated elevators. His uncle was ambushed coming off an elevator, so he told himself to never use them in a public place. He walked up to the fourth floor level and went to the front desk. He asked for Dr. Phillips. He was paged over the intercom. He came walking down the hallway with a smile on his face. He extended his hand as he approached Honcho. They shook hands as they greeted each other. "How's it going?" he asked. "It's going okay, but what was so urgent? Honcho asked. "Is everything okay with my pops? "Actually, everything is fine," Dr. Phillips said reassuringly. "We ran some tests and the results were great." Your father is most likely going to wake up at any moment. He can hear everything that's going on around him. He's just got to figure out how to bring himself back. His brain activity is all over the place, but I promise you, he will be up and alert in no time. The part of his brain that was hit somehow didn't receive the type of damage we thought. His brain is fully functional and he could likely wake up any day now. I can't promise you his memory will be a hundred percent, but from the tests, it should not be an issue. If anything new comes up, I will give you a call right away." "Thank you, Dr. Phillips. Have a good evening," Honcho said as he walked towards his father's room.

Later That Evening.

CASH MONEY CHICKS.

Tiff finished packing her overnight bag. She was waiting for Preston. He called and told her he was headed that way. She asked Tee and Lee where the car was that Tiny let them use earlier. "It's parked at the clubhouse," Lee said. "Why do you ask that? she asked. "Because Preston is on his way over to pick me up and I don't want him seeing that car anywhere near here, especially after y'all said someone walked up on you while you were staking the place out. Luckily, he didn't spot you." Tiff said. "How could he? The windows are super dark," Lee responded. "Well, what did y'all find out so far? "He stopped at 11 different locations, so we have to pretty much sit on each one until we figure out which ones are the stash houses. He then drove to a storage unit location, and his car has been at the same location for the past three days." "Do you think he located the tracking device?" Tee asked. "Ain't no way," said Lee. "He's driving his Hummer, so he must have left the Lambo at the storage spot while he took care of something and he didn't want to attract attention. That's the only logical explanation for the car to be sitting for three days," said Tiff.

Their conversation was interrupted by the sound of the doorbell. It was Preston. She buzzed him in. Once he made it to the second floor, he walked to their suite, 708. He started to knock, but the door flew open, and Tiff was standing there holding a plate of strawberries. He laughed. "Aren't you forgetting something? Preston asked. "You know, the hot chocolate." "It is inside my bag. All we've got to do is warm it up," Tiff said. "Hello ladies," he said to Lee and Tee when he stepped inside to grab Tiff's bags for her. Lee's freaky ass was thinking about where she could put the strawberry and watch Preston eat and suck them out of her pussy. She said "I want to go." Preston stopped in mid stride, turned around and looked at Tiff with that look like *hell yeah*.

Tiff wasn't in the mood to share tonight. She said "next time Sis." Lee said "sharing is caring," and they all started laughing as they walked out of the door. Preston said "you ladies have a good night." "I would say the same to you," Tee said, "but from the looks of things, you guys are going to have a great night," he winked at her and closed the door on his way out.

A few days later, Tee and Lee were sitting down the street from one of the locations that the tracking device hit on. There was heavy traffic, so they knew it was a trap spot. They moved on to the next location. It was pretty much the same demo - heavy traffic and plenty of people coming and going. They figured they would try one more today. They would pick up again tomorrow. As they were pulling up to the third one, they saw a familiar face. It was a dude who was at the very first spot. He was retrieving three duffel bags out of the backseat of a Honda. It appeared they may have found the stash house. One of them at least. After the dude entered, another car pulled up. It was the guy who we just saw at the second spot. He also retrieved a couple of duffle bags and entered the same spot. Shortly after, both of them came out empty-handed. They spoke for a minute, got in their vehicles and pulled off. "Bingo!" Lee said. "It definitely is a stash house. Okay, we will get to the other addresses tomorrow and see what else we can find out. My gut is telling me there is at least one more stash house," Tee said. "Let's call it a night," Lee said. "We can finish our detective work in the morning. I am hungry and tired."

Chapter 36

RICO.

 Rico was facing 18 and life. Shit was looking real bleak, but he was standing firm. They came at him with all types of deals. "Give us your supplier," they asked and Rico would piss them off by saying "give me your wife and we might be able to work something out," which would earn him a few gut shots and a handful of slaps across the face. He never broke or folded, and they would just have him escorted back to his pod. Rico would have loved to go home, but he would never turn rat/snitch. His name is his brand and he stands on 100%. All a man is born with it his word and his balls, so f*** the Feds, and Rico had already put the word on snitching ass Lenny. It's just a matter of time before somebody collects that bounty. There is $100,000 to whoever cuts this police ass white boy like fish. Rico goes to sentencing next month. He took a cop; ain't no way he can go to trial with a star witness. That's work, and he just wants to get his time and get transferred to his parent institution. He was ready to get the f*** out of CCA. He had been in this b**** a little over a year. He got Gunner out there cleaning his money by opening up more clubs, restaurants, a few barber shops and hella salons. Big Moby was pushing the f*** out the rock, and pulling up at will draining three pointers at will, Everything is cool nigga, just ready to get the ball on the road. He heard through the grapevine the youngin New Bag got a real connect, and he's flooding the city with some of the best s*** the City has seen. Everybody gets a turn, Rico said to himself. It's Youngin's turn, and when it's time for him to exit, I hope he makes better decisions than I did.

EL ROSSO

El Rosso was about to pull a move that no one ever would have thought of. He was going to have Julio kidnapped and held for ransom, but he would eventually let him go only to have them follow him right to the boss himself. Then he would go in for the kill. See, Julio is very smart in the game we play, but he is also very careless. He also travels without any guards. He's always at his diner, and he feels he can't be touched. In this lifestyle, anybody can be touched. El Rosso had flown his son to Mexico so he could break everything down so he understood. He was pacing in his office when his phone rang. "Hello, I'm here." Hassani announced. The jet had landed okay. "I will see you shortly," said El Rosso.

Forty-five minutes later, Hassani walked through the door of the 30 million dollar estate escorted by several armed guards. He felt like a prisoner, but little did he know, these men worked for him. He was about to find out just why his father sent for him after all these years. "You have a seat, my son. Do you want a drink?" El Rosso asked. "Yes, I could really use one right about now" Hassani said. "I would like to know why it was so very important that I fly all the way to Mexico." "Listen and listen close," El Rosso began. "I do own several multi-million dollar companies, but I started the companies with drug money my son." "So, you're telling me you're a drug dealer?" Hassani asked. "So I am the son of a drug dealer?" "No," El Rosso explained. "I am telling you that you are the leader of the Lamia cartel, and since you're my firstborn son, that makes you second in charge. Your little brother and sister were kidnapped and murdered a month ago by the Aztec cartel." "My little brother and sister? I didn't even know I had a little brother and sister." Hassani said. "I know, and I'm sorry for that," El Rosso said. "But your family needs you. "My family? You must be joking!" Hassani retorted. "Right now you can be mad or upset, I understand, but it's time for you to take your seat at the table." El Rosso continued, "You are a Lamia. It runs through your veins. This is a lot to take in at such short notice. Look, I have a plan, but it won't work without you. I need you son. The family needs you. A team is only as good as their leader, so be a good leader and lead your family to victory. If not for me, do it for your brother and sister." Hassani said "show me to my room and give me a minute to think." El Rosso watched as Hassani walked out of the office. The look on his face gave El Rosso his answer. He had seen that look before and it was a look of pure evil. He didn't know what was going on inside his son's head, but he would soon find out.

EL ROSSO, JR.

Hassani was lying across the bed staring at the ceiling with a million and one things going through his head. The first was that he couldn't believe his dad never told him he had a brother and a sister. If he had been in their lives, he could have protected them from this mayhem. He never got a chance to meet them, and now he never would. The more he thought about it, the more his hatred was building for everyone tied to the Aztec cartel. His father called him here to take his seat at the table as second-in-command, but he was going to take his father's seat at the head of Lamia cartel. Anyone who begged to differ would be murdered on the spot. See, Hassani didn't grow up in Mexico around the murderers, the trafficking of metro tons of drugs, the kidnapping and mini car bombings and being under pressure at all times. He grew up in the states and got the best education money could buy. He was a thinker, something his pops wasn't. With his brains and the blood of El Rosso pumping through his veins, he planned to bring the Aztec Cartel to its knees.

First thing the next morning, he would gather all the information he could pertaining to Aztec and set up a team to watch their every move from afar. Once he had their pattern down pat, he would snatch someone of high standards, hit them where it hurt, their pockets first and find out where their operations were located and destroy them completely. They were in a deadly lifestyle. If you made a mistake, it would cost you or the ones around you. His father had already made that mistake, and it cost not just him, but he cheated Hassani out of a chance to have a life with his little brother and sister. Every move he made will cost his opponent dearly. This was a game of chess. If he loses, he dies. It was time to push his pawns. He lay there until he drifted off to sleep.

HECTOR.

Hector was highly upset once the news reached him. One of the pickup locations had been hit. They murdered everyone in the house and cleaned out all the stash units each holding 200 kilos. Hector knew El Rosso was behind it, but what he didn't know was it was not El'Rosso himself calling the shots, it was his illegitimate son from the states. His son was more strategic and more of a thinker. Hector called for a meeting at the farm. It was very intense because Hector was known to shoot at the drop of a dime. A few of his own men faced that fate. Hector wanted the farm heavily guarded at all times 24 hours a day. He also wanted all the shipments rerouted and the drop points changed. He even wanted a new stash house put into play. He felt this first hit was just the beginning of many more, so he had to plan ahead.

He called Julio to let him know to be cautious and stop traveling without guards, and to switch up his routine. If anyone did their homework, Julio would be the easiest target out of the top three in charge. After the meeting, Hector was en route to his hideaway.

He stopped traveling to and from his estate. He didn't want to be caught by having a set pattern, so he switched up his whole operation. He now believed he was a few steps ahead, or so he thought. He had no clue that he, Chi-Chi and Julio were being followed for the past two weeks now.

JULIO.

Julio was on the phone with Zenru. Zenru was calling to let him know he received the load at the drop point, and he looked forward to doing more business in the future. As Julio was ending his call, a gentleman walked into his diner, took a seat and started looking over the menu. After a few moments, Hassani waved the waiter over and placed his order. He caught Julio looking at him and put on his best smile. "It's a lovely day," he said. "I can't get enough of this weather." Once Julio spoke, he relaxed and indulged in a conversation with the American. Little did he know, he was having a conversation with El Rosso's first born son who lived here in the states.

Julio's phone rang and Hassani returned to his cup of coffee still waiting on his food. It was Hector on the other end giving Julio an update on what was going on and to suggest that he switch up his routine until they put an end to this Lamia thing. When he got off the phone he and the American customer picked up where they left off. "So, where are the hotspots? I'm from the East Coast. I just moved here a month ago, job-related, of course," Hassani said, trying to bait Julio, and he fell for it. I go, to this club over on 1114 in Lincoln. It's an upscale spot that goes Sunday to Sunday, no off days. One of my favorite spots," Julio said. Hassani said "I have definitely got to check it out. I've been so busy at work, I haven't had time to get out and mingle, so that's what I plan on doing all this weekend starting today." "Well, you are definitely in the right place for it. Miami is like Vegas, just minus the casinos. We never sleep, 24-hour clubs. It's the place to live life, but it's also very expensive," said Julio. After Hassani finished his meal, he thanked Julio for the advice and told him the food was great. "Till next time," he said with a smile as he exited the diner. Phase one of his plan was complete. Julio was feeling good. He loved interacting with the American, but this American was not who he portrayed himself to be.

Chapter 37

Back In Cleveland.

NEW BAG.

New Bag was putting that dog in the street like it was legal. He even gave his s*** a name. Everybody in the City was looking for that s*** drop man as he slid through down the way to meet one of his niggas who had the bricks on smash. See, Wade was no average hustler. When Kevin Gates made that song 'Out the Mud' he should have had a picture of Wade on the cover. He wasn't just getting to the bag, he was getting a whole bunch of bagssssssss, if you catch my drift. New Bag pulled up to the one-way off 46th and Outhwaite. He parked his Maserati behind a Porsche Cayenne, jumped out and walked toward a group of dudes. As they conversed, a hard-ass red Jag truck came down the street. Everybody turned to look at the vehicle. A few young boys was like "look at this clown ass n****." Typical broke hating nigga shit. New Bag chopped it up for a few minutes then pulled off.

One reason Wade was copping from him was because his hook just got popped, and he ain't got around to going outta town to find another plug. Truth be told though, Wade got way more money than New Bag, and the City knows that. New Bag was raking in that paper like it was falling off trees. He was making so much money that he was running out of places to hide it. That nigga Rico had the nerve to call his phone after he cut him off. New Bag was feeling himself. He answered and said "if it ain't about money, then I don't got time for it. Since you locked in the Feds, I don't see this call being beneficial to me. What's up?" Rico was hot. He didn't know how to respond so he just hung up. That's what I thought, New Bag said to himself. Shidd, everybody gets a turn. It is just what you're going to do when you get your turn. New Bag was going to make the most of his run, and he had his own hook. No lookouts, no handouts. He got to a bag off the muscle from robbing and shooting s***, to being pulled into the fold. He made all the right choices, now the City is his playground. Only thing better than the bag is a new bag, remember that.

RICO.

Damn, white boy Lenny did his thing on Rico. They gave him 20 years just on hearsay, and the $325,000 in his condo. No drugs or guns were found. Rico was transferred to Federal Correctional Institution McKean, located in Bradford, Pennsylvania, he got lucky and went to a medium instead of the United States Penitentiary. As soon as he hit the compound and walked out of quartermaster, so many different niggas was calling his name, Mad Max-Rico. As soon as he made it to the other side of the walkway there was a group of Cleveland dudes. It was like they knew he was coming. N***** was asking if he needed anything but he told them he was good. A few of them already had a bag put together for him.

As they walked towards their units, one of them asked him if he had his paperwork. Paperwork is everything about your case, and if you have a 5K1 anywhere in your paperwork, that meant you snitched on someone or cooperated with the government. He looked like he was offended. "Hell yeah I got my paperwork. I'm a stand-up guy. I will never bend, break or fold. My name is Mad Max. Niggas who knew him from the streets was like, 'my nigga one of the realest niggas you will ever meet.' He had a heavy plug, and he was putting that s*** out in the streets. His dude Devin asked "what unit are you on?" "I'm on CB." Rico answered. "That's the unit me, Big Heavy, Mojizzle and Convert Boo on." Rico walked into the pod holding his s*** and the CO told him what cell he was assigned to. It was located five doors down from the CO's office.

After he got all his shit put away in his cell, he went to go to the yard, but he couldn't. They only let you move from one location to another every hour. That is a ten-minute move, so you have ten minutes to get where you are going. Being out of place once they end the ten minute move is a fosho write up. He dipped out to the gym-yard. That b**** was packed like it was a family cookout. Mexicans were in one section of the yard, MS-thirteen was all on the handball court, Ohio niggas were all under the Pavilion, and DC niggas were playing the bleachers. A few New York cats were playing, the yard and the bleachers. This s*** is totally different from the State. As soon as he walked into the gym, Mojizzle from the Six was like "Damn, I heard what happened. We can't win with all these whole ass n***** telling. "Man, who are you telling!" Rico said. , man who you telling, Rico's crazy ass wasted no time, "So how do this spot get down? What CO bringing it in?" "Hell naw" Mojizzle replied, "it's in here though, but we're dancing out there on visits. You can only get so much in at a time." "Shidd," Rico said, "I'm about to change all that. Give me ninety days. I'm a have this bitch loaded and wide-open, trust me, my nigga, we might be on lock but the hustle doesn't stop." Mojizzle chucked, "You're talkin my language. You know I live for this s***. I heard they got the white boy that told on you in the SHU. They didn't put a separation on you two?" "I guess not. You know how the Feds do - use you up and then throw you to the wolves, and I'm definitely a wolf." "How long he got in that b****?" Rico asked. "I don't know. They say he poked his cellie up after they transferred him from CCA. The nigga turned his 20-year sentence into life," Mojizzle said. "Shidd, that doesn't matter. He was a dead man anyway. I put a hundred on his head," Rico said. "Damn you loaded that like that?   I can get one of these DC niggas like Ten to put the play down for you. All I got to do is holler at my nigga. Word is he runs the DC car. He a cool ass nigga. I met him back in 2005 when I was down in DC kicking it." Mojizzle said. "S*** make that happen ASAP!" Rico said. "Soon as that b**** as Nigga get out of the hole, I want him put down like a dog that bit his master. "Say no more, it's done. Let me get back to the unit so I can jump on the jack." Jack means the phone. He was headed back to the unit. He needed to make a few calls. He thought to himself, *this place is a gold mind I just gotta tap into.*

WHITE BOY LENNY.

Lenny was going crazy in the hole. It was going on ten months, and every inmate seems to know he's a rat. He's been getting all types of threats, and to make matters worse, he's broke. The Feds took everything, and people ran off with the money they didn't know about. It's all bad! He just wants to get out this hole. One thing for sure, the first person to approach him about being a snitch, he's going to put down a mean demo because he refuses to live in fear. If people have a problem with him telling on Rico, they better keep it to themselves. He has a life sentence with nothing to lose. He's going to be known as Lenny the Snitch and Lenny that would gut your ass.

The only f***** up part is he doesn't know Rico was just transferred to McKean today. A black guy named Zip was walking down the tear to hit the showers and stopped at Lenny's cell door and said "the only thing better than a pussy is some new pussy, and guess who the pussy is? I will be waiting for you when you get out the SHU" "F*** you nigga. I won't have you waiting too long," Lenny yelled. Move along, said the CO. All you heard were inmates screaming up and down the range. Being locked in a small ass cell 24 hours a day is hell minus the fire.

TRUCKER J.

I was walking around the old small junkyard I just bought. A little touch-up here and there and it would be perfect for what I'm trying to do. I walked back into the office. It had two small rooms, a bathroom, tiny kitchen area and lounge. I called William boys. That's my close friend who owns his own business. He is one of the coolest in the City. He arrived thirty minutes later and I showed him around and told him my plan. He said he would need around two weeks. We shook hands and I wrote him a check for twenty thousand. I lingered around a little longer after he left just picturing how everything would be when it's done. I had to make an appointment to go see three rigs, three dump trucks, two dump trailers and a cargo trailer. The total for all of that would be $290,000. I wrote a check and everything was scheduled to be delivered to my truck yard tomorrow morning.

I headed home but I stopped at Flowerama on the corner of Libby and Warrensville. I grabbed my wife, a huge teddy bear and five dozen roses. I pulled into the driveway and came in the side door. My twins took off towards the living room yelling "Mommy, Mommy, Daddy got you balloons and flowers," so before I walked into the living room she was already smiling, holding a book in her hand she was reading. She jumped up and damn near knocked me down trying to hug and kiss me. I looked into her eyes and said "I love you. You complete me in every way possible, and I'm glad you chose me to spend your life with." She started crying, and the twins asked her "Mommy, why are you crying? What's wrong?" Toya and I couldn't help but to chuckle at how cute their faces were . They were confused to see her first smiling and then crying. I told her I wanted to show her something very important in the morning. Me, Toya and the boys stayed up late watching movies and talking. My boys are growing up, so what I bought today was worth every penny, because now I can hire people to drive and allow me to spend more time with my family. Toya is going to be so happy.

The next morning I woke up and cooked breakfast. We all bathed, dressed and headed out the door. In the passenger seat sat the teddy bear I bought yesterday. I put the boys in their car seats. Toya climbed in the front and was all smiles and thanking me for the bear. We headed to the truck yard. As soon as we pulled up into the truck yard, every truck I picked out yesterday was lined up and parked in a straight line. Glen and his crew were inside doing their thing. I said "come on baby," and she said "I will wait while you go look at some trucks." I said "baby those are our trucks for Frank's Trucking company." She looked at the sign realizing this was the surprise. She jumped out and walked around the trucks. She saw Glen come out of the office front door. He asked "James, how do you want the kitchen and the office done?". I looked at Toya and said to Glen "You need to ask the owner, and pointed to my wife." She started crying again. She looked at the twins like *mommy is happy. These are happy tears!* She followed Glen into his office. The twins and I walked towards the trucks. The twins said Daddy can we get inside of that one, and I said you can get in all of them, you and your brother own all this this is all yours one day you will be controlling all this, so you both have to learn all you can about the business and guess who's going to teach you, you are Daddy they both said and in that moment I knew I made the right decision,

Glen finally came out of the office with Toya, and said "it's going to take me a few extra weeks to do everything this crazy-ass woman wants done, and I'm going to need some more money." "How much more?" I asked. "Another twenty thousand," Glen said. Toya looked at me and she said, "You said I'm the boss." I pulled out my checkbook and wrote a check for thirty thousand. "This is in case she changes anything else. You know how women are," and we all laughed. Toya looked at me and asked where the boys were. The Twins stuck their heads out of the window of one of the dump trucks and said "Up here Mommy."

BIG MOBY.

Moby was sliding through the Fleet area. There had been a lot of s*** going on. His one spot got hit and they took K to jail because somebody OD'd in her house. She refused to cooperate so they locked her up. She was realer than a lot of these so-called street niggas. His phone rang. He wasn't in the mood to talk, but it was Rico. He pushed five to accept the call. "What up Nephew?" "Shit was good," Rico said. "I got somebody that's going to call you. You need to meet him and give him $50,000 and a brick of dog but not pure. Put a two on it. I ain't trying to kill nobody! Next, give him a brick of coke and three pounds of cush. You got all that, huh?" "Yeah, I got it," Moby said. "I see the hustle don't stop, but are you sure about this?" "I'm sure," Rico replied. "How are things moving out there for you?" "It's all love on my end," Moby said. "My only problem is where to hide all this f****** money, for real, I didn't know you fell across a connect this heavy. I know you got some millions buried somewhere." "You can say something like that." Rico said. They both went back and forth for a while, then Rico said he had to go. "It's count time, but before I go, make sure you put five cell phones in there and do not forget the chargers." "I got you." Moby said before they hung up.

Chapter 38

EL ROSSO, JR.

Hassani was back in the States for a reason. He was on a mission to befriend Julio and eventually have him kidnapped. He knew it was going to take some time and a lot of stops by the diner, but he had a few things going in his favor; one being he was born in the States and two, Julio had no idea that he was El Rosso's son. He personally put together a hit squad to just watch and trail Julio, to follow his every move. He found out Julio hit the upscale club twice a week, always on the same two days. So Hassani would make sure he was at the Club this Friday, and he was definitely putting on a show acting like a drunk American, having a great time and spending money. The very moment Julio walked in the Club, his men outside called and told him the package had arrived and ended the call. He walked to the bar and bought a cranberry and orange juice mix, and went out onto the dance floor. He started dancing with a woman who had been flirting with him all night. After five songs, he and the lady made it back to the bar. Julio walked over and greeted him. "I see you made it to see the Club. How do you like it?" asked Julio. "Oh, it's very nice and beautiful women all over. My type of party. Hey, there is an after party at one of my condos and you're welcome to join us. You can even ride over with me if you're up for it. "Cool!" He thought to himself - bingo! Things falling into place way sooner than planned. "Yes, I would love to. Let me know when you're about to leave," Hassani said. "Okay my friend, you and your lady friend's drinks are on me. My buddy owns the place."

JULIO.

Julio's driver was pulling into the parking garage. There were around 14 other vehicles in tow. Everyone who was with Julio had access to enter the garage, so the hit squad had no problem gaining access. They just casually drove in like they were a part of the party. They pulled all the way to the rear of the garage and killed their engines. The people exiting their cars and SUVs never even noticed them. Julio and his few passengers all climbed out and headed for the elevators. Amongst the group was Hassani and his lady friend. Thirty-two individuals all piled into three different elevators. Once they reached the Penthouse, it was breathtaking. There was a mini bar with a sexy ass bartender. It had a huge jacuzzi, and even had a dance floor area that sat dead smack in the middle of the room. Before you knew it, there was a drug buffet. There were bowls full of coke, weed and even some crystal meth,

Julio was definitely entertaining his guests. There was a maid walking around filling everyone's glasses and a cook taking orders. People were sitting around eating. While others were putting cocaine up their nose, Hassani sat watching Julio's every move. Every now and then, he would raise his glass, and looking in my direction, toast to the good life. Julio was telling a couple of sexy ladies to get into the jacuzzi. They stripped down. It was really on! The women were pouring bubbly all over each other and it looked like soft porn. Hassani went to the bathroom to call down to the hit squad. It's going to be a long night. As soon as he steps off the elevator, snatch him and kill the driver, but dump his body somewhere else. The person on the other end of the phone said "Copy."

Back in Cleveland.

GUNNER.

S*** was looking lovely from where Gunner was sitting. He just wished his nigga Rico was with him. They gave his Nigga twenty years.

Damn! One f****** up decision can alter your whole life, but my nigga is a stand up dude. He took it on the chin, and he knew he got a real motherfucka in his corner. Every time I'm on the phone with my nigga, he seems to be in good spirits, and he still being Rico, talking about he's sitting on a gold mine. Crazy ass nigga going to hustle until God Allah calls him home. It f***** me up when the nigga FaceTimed me today. He already got a C in his pocket. We chopped it for a minute then he said he would hit me back.

I really didn't want to get up today. I figured I would hang around the house with my wife and little angel. I have been so busy getting my clubs and restaurants up and going. I really ain't had time to really enjoy myself. My wife was upstairs. "What kind of eggs do you want," she asked. I heard my daughter tell her "daddy wants a sunny side up." All I could do was laugh. My wife called my name again, and I said "you heard my baby, sunny side up." It felt good living on the right side of the tracks. There was piece of mind, no matter what a nigga says. I believe every nigga wants this. They just don't know how to transition, and some just are scared of change. Me walking away from the street was the best decision I ever made in my life. I just regret that Rico didn't make the same.

NEW BAG.

The world is mine and everything in it! New Bag was laid up in his king size bed listening to music while his b**** and her girlfriend both sucked him off at the same damn time. Yeah, he was living like a king. MeMe put the head of his dick into her mouth and played with it with her tongue ring, while KeKe straddled his face and began to grind her hips slow. He stuck his tongue up into her wet fat pussy and spread her ass cheeks apart. She was holding his head and really f****** his mouth. He felt Mimi straddle his dick. It was warm as she eased down on his manhood. She lifted up and brought her ass down with force over and over until she said she was about to cum. She started going fast. KeKe had already nutted twice in his mouth. After Mimi came all over his dick, he slapped both of their asses so they could get up. He positioned himself behind KeKe and spread her ass cheeks, sliding his dick in her pussy and f****** her like a man on a mission. While he was f****** her brains out, MeMe lay down in front of her and KeKe started sucking her pussy something crazy. Two hours later, they were still going at it. The pills they popped last night hadn't let them sleep yet. New Bag was eating their pussy back and forth, watching them nut over and over. He loved the way their toes curled, the faces they made and them telling him to *eat that pussy!* "Oh my God, I'm cumming," said KeKe. They were chasing nut after nut. One of them would nut and then the next. They did this nearly all day long.

BIG MOBY.

Moby was walking out of K's back door on 55th and Fleet when two little niggas ran up the driveway with no masks on, holding guns bigger than them. The taller one was the one in charge, because he was the only one talking. He shouted "where it's at nigga? Don't make me bust you." Moby being older and not new to this type of situation, said "it's in my pocket." They said "get it and move slow." Moby reached in his pocket with his other hand still in the air. He knew they were young, because they didn't walk him to his truck, which is where two kilos of dog was at about $140,000, so he wasn't even mad. He gave them the $12,000 had on him. Their eyes got big as saucers. They thought they had hit the jackpot. They told him to lay down and he did. They took off running and Moby got up laughing thinking to himself, another day in the hood. Moby thought to himself, *when I see those little niggas though, I'm going to teach them when you play a grown man's game there are grown man consequences, and I'm definitely going to welcome them to manhood!*

Moby jumped in his truck and pulled off. He was headed to meet the CO who Rico got to bring the pack in for him at FCI McKean. First it was a dude, now he got him meeting the dude and a woman on different days of the same week. Rico must be flooding that b**** like he in the streets, Moby thought. As he pulled into the parking lot of Walmart, speaking of the devil, Rico was calling his phone – well, he was FaceTiming him. "What's up youngin?" "Shit, everything good on my end, but how shit go on your end," Moby asked. Rico said, "I'm waiting for the old girl to pull up right now. What's up with you though?" "Everything, everything, better believe it. I'm making a killing in this b**** . I got this b**** wide-open, that's what's up." Rico said "just be careful. You know with success comes envy and hate, even when you feeding niggas, they feel like they should be getting more than they are getting, then greed sets in and then the fuckary. Just watch how and who you f*** with my nephew. But let me hit you back, your people just pulled up." "Okay, but let me hit you up unc."

F.C.I.
MCKEAN

Lenny was finally released from the SHU and housed on unit AA. He was walking across the compound to the quartermaster to get his property. Rico was walking across also and didn't want Lenny to see him, so he ducked off into the library. Once he was past the school, Rico shot up to the unit to tell his nigga Mojizzle to put the plan into motion. That rat Lenny was out of the hole. He grabbed his bag and to his unit. A few Cleveland n***** was shocked that both he and Rico were at McKean, with Lenny telling on Rico and all. As he walked past the group of guys, one of them said "ain't that the n**** Lenny from the West Side?" "Yeah," someone responded. "That's him. He told on the nigga Rico. He is hot. Hot meant you snitched on somebody. Lenny continued walking as if he didn't hear them, and finally made it to his cell.

When he got back to his cell, he saw his cellie lying down reading a book, Without looking up, he said "you got a week to find another cell. I don't fuck with rats." Lenny dropped his shit and said "you better go find another cell then nigga." The guy started to get up, but he saw the two large shanks in Lenny hands, and he looked at Lenny and his eyes said it all. Either kill or be killed. Dude was locked up on a drug charge, so he wasn't about to take it there. He looked at Lenny at the knives in his hands and said "it ain't that serious." He lay back down and got back into his book. Lenny looked at dude and said "it is that serious, and stay the fuck out my way." He started unpacking his shit and putting his clothes in his locker. Someone opened the cell door and announced that it was chow time.

After his cellie was gone, Lenny put his two knives on his hip and walked out of the cell and followed the crowd towards the chow hall. *Fuck it,* he thought to himself. *Let's get this show on the road.* There were two long lines that led into the chow hall. Once inside, it was loud and packed. He walked through the line with his head up. Once he got his food, he went to sit down and one the Cleveland niggas said "you got to sit somewhere else. These tables are for real niggas only, not rat ass niggas like you." Before he could respond, four niggas pulled out shanks/knives and one of them said "we heard you push that knife. Shidd, we do too." Lenny looked around. It seemed like every Ohio nigga was looking at him. He walked to another part of the chow hall and found a seat. He hated that he ever cooperated with the Feds. Shit was all bad. When he thought it couldn't get any worse, Rico walked past him smiling and winked. He thought he was tripping until he seen Rico and a group of DC niggas looking at him pointing.

After chow, Lenny walked to the gym. He was hanging in the yard when one of his homies from his hood walked up on him. "Yo Lenny, whats up?" Lil' Pete said. "Everybody is saying you told on the young boy from Fleet." The look Lenny gave his nigga said it all. "Damn, for real man?" "Yeah, I did some fucked up shit and the Feds played me." Lenny replied. "You better be careful. Rico got this bitch on smash," Lil' Pete warned. "Don't anything move unless he says so, and he's only been here a few months. He put money on your head. Don't trust nobody, and I mean nobody. "Bet," Lenny said. They dapped and Lenny walked to the gym to use the restroom. As soon as he walked into the bathroom, Ice and Prem ran down on him. Little did they know Lenny had peeped them following him around the yard for the last 30 minutes, so when he went into the restroom he hid behind the door with both of his knives in hand, ready to strike. As they ran into the bathroom and past the door, Lenny ran up and hit Ice three times in the neck. He was dead before he hit the floor. Prem turned around when he heard Ice scream, but it was too late. Lenny had the drop on him. Fighting for his life, he moved swiftly and put all his power into his swing. He stuck Prem dead smack in the middle of his chest cavity, an inch away from his heart. Two more vicious blows to his midsection and Lenny turned and dipped up out of there.

He stood by the gate waiting on the 10 minute move. He shot back to his unit, hid his knives and took a shower to wash off the blood. He was walking to his cell as the jail was being put on lock down. Everyone was saying Prem and Ice were killed in the gym area. Lenny walked to his cell and shut his cell door. Rico was just hearing about Ice and Prem and he thought, how the f*** did Lenny pull that off! Back to the drawing board, he said to himself. Lenny was known for being a snitch, but now he was known for getting busy. He definitely will push that knife and the whole compound knew it

Chapter 39

JULIO.

Julio still couldn't believe he allowed himself to be snatched. It's like he walked right into the trap. Now he sat blindfolded, beaten, starved and naked in the empty warehouse. The thing that's throwing him off is that one of the voices he hears is so familiar. He just couldn't put a face on it. He knew it would come to him eventually. Days turned into weeks. He felt he was on the verge of death when one day someone brought a bag of food from his diner and it hit him. That voice - it's the f****** American from the diner. Now it's starting to make sense. The diner visits, then the Club - all the s*** was planned and I didn't see it.

The American walked into the warehouse where Julio was being held and greeted him, "My friend, how's it going? You see, I picked up your favorite. They say you haven't been at the diner going on two weeks now." Julio begins cussing and yelling all kinds of threats. "You m***********, you are a dead man, he shouted. "Hey, hey now, slow down with that getting all worked up. You are going to need your energy my friend. Either you're going to help me or you're going to die sitting right there. I promise you that. Let me let you in on a little secret. My name is El Rosso, Jr., the new leader of the Lamia Cartel. Julio realized just how fucked he was. If he decided to help El'Rosso, Jr., Hector and the Aztec's will murder him, but if he didn't, he knew he would never leave this place alive. "What is it you need my help with?" Julio asked. El Rosso replied, "Everything. I want to know everything. I'm going to kill the head of your

Cartel with your help or without it. But if you help me, you will live to take a seat at the head of the table, and you will stay out my way." "Even if you kill Hector, I'm not next in line, Chi-Chi is," Julio said. "Oh, so I guess he has to die as well," El Rosso replied. "Do we have a deal, or is this warehouse going to be your tomb, my friend? We have a 'fuck' don't think too long. I am not a patient man." El Rosso, Jr. said.

HECTOR.

Hector was just informed by Chi-Chi that he hadn't been able to get hold of Julio for over three weeks now, and he hadn't been back to the diner either. "Something just isn't right. That's not like him. He loves that diner, and I know something bad has happened." Chi-Chi said. "What is Louis saying?" Hector asked. "Only thing he said was this guy who just moved to Miami for work had been stopping by the diner lot, and he and Julio got kind of cool. Then Julio went missing. The guy stopped by once and ordered something to eat, but ordered it to go and he had never done that before. He said it's for a friend, my good friend. That's what he and Julio used to say to each other," Louis said. "Chi-Chi, I need you to go to the states and figure this s*** out. Something isn't right. We just got to figure out what it is. Two more drop points were hit this week. They are trying to clean us out, that is not even El Rosso's way of doing things. I think he's working with someone else for backup. We have to strike back, and I mean now. We've got to find out where their stash houses are. We are not going to rob them, we are going to blow them up! Matter of fact, put a million in the streets. Let all the gangs know we are hiring guns. We are going to stop all of Lamia's cash flow. Hire every gang around Mexico. I don't care how much it costs. I'm ready to put an end to this war, once and for all." "I'm on it boss. I will call you once my plane lands in the states," Chi-Chi said. "Very well," Hector said. "Be careful my good friend."

EL ROSSO, JR.

Hassani exited his private jet in Mexico. The plan he put into play had been going well. His father was surprised how Hassani had stepped up, and not just claimed a seat at the table, but he claimed his father's seat. El Rosso stepped down to see if his son had what it takes to run the family business. Little did he know, Hassani had what it took and more. He wasn't just going to wipe out Hector and Chi-Chi, he was going to also kill Julio. But he was saving the best for last, his father El Rosso. Once he was en route to the estate that he was now the overseer of, he called his father. "I'm back in Mexico and will be pulling up shortly," he said. "How did it go back in the states?" El Rosso asked. "Better than we planned, or should I

say better than I planned." Hassani answered.
"So where is Julio and what did you find out"
What information did he give you?" El Rosso
was ready to cause mayhem. All this planning
and waiting was not how he did things, but he
was no longer the one in charge. Hassani was
the one calling the shots now. "I will be there
shortly and will fill you in on everything,"
Hassani answered.

Back in Miami.

MARGIELA.

Margelia was pounding with the pack. There
were about 300 of them. They had Ocean
Drive lined up with some of the coldest bikes in
the City. Margiela has not been on his bike in
a while. It felt good to get out on the open road
and get gas. He was a speed demon, and he
loved the rush it gave him. They were just

riding and letting their presence be felt throughout Miami. From the beach to the ghetto, they were headed to the Clubhouse. They had a group riding in from Detroit, so tonight was going to be super-packed with over 300 bikes on the scene. They pulled up to the Clubhouse and everybody backed their bikes in. It was a sight to see. They piled into the club and it instantly started going. Tiny, being the second in charge, was always at Margelia's right side. They were like brothers from another. Tiny spotted Tee at the bar and went over to say what's up to her. The fellows from Detroit arrived. They got the royalty treatment since they're from out of town. That's how it goes in the motorcycle world. Everybody had their colors on. A few Patriots didn't have colors, but they knew the demo. When we do roll call shut the f****** or we will lock the doors and shut you the f******. Big Bruce was the leader of the Most Wanted MC located in Detroit. He was a cool ass dude that Margelia met years back when he had a breakdown in the D. They had shown him hella love and treated him with the utmost respect. That s*** formed a friendship strong and solid only the real can relate to.

CASH MONEY CHICKS.

Lee and Tee were ready to pull off the move, but they had to wait for Tiff to give the okay.

She had started to really like this dude Preston. Forgetting that he was their target, Lee was laying across the couch and Tee was sitting in the Lazy Boy. "So, what are we waiting for? Everything is in place. We know the whole routine, all the stash spots, and even a few dope spots. Tiff needs to get her nose out of dude's ass already," Tee said. "We need to holler at her as soon as she comes back. Ain't no more waiting or putting it off. We will be making this happen this coming week. If we got to put Preston down, so be it," Lee said. "I feel you, but if we got to kill him let me f*** him first. I need to see what that mouth and that dick do." They both burst out laughing. "If busting nuts is all you think about," Tee said, "If snorting coke all you think about," Lee said, "then touch." she said. "Where is Tiff anyway?" "Where you think she is - with Preston. "Do you want me to call her and see what time she's coming back?" Tee asked. "Nope, but when she does get here, I'm definitely letting her know what's up though." Lee replied.

TIFF.

Tiff was out and about with Preston. They were at the beach just chilling and Preston said "I want to introduce you to someone important to me, but they are in a mind frame that is unstable right now, but they are getting better day by day. What do you say" he asked. "If it's important to you, then it's important to me baby," she said rubbing his back. They lay out in the sun talking for hours before heading into the beach house to bath and get dressed. Once they were dressed, they headed to a nice restaurant to have a bite to eat. After that, they were headed to someplace so Tiff could meet that someone Preston held close to his heart.

HEAD HONCHO.

Head Honcho was putting his plan into motion. He is taking Tiff to the hospital with him while he visits his father. He couldn't find out if the triplets were the Cash Money Chicks, so he figured he would take her with him. He knew his father could hear everything. If his machine starts to go crazy when he hears Tiff's voice, *bingo!* He would also pay very close attention to Tiff and see if her expression or body language changed at any point during the visit. So, let the games begin. They were getting closer and closer to the hospital. He looked over at Tiff and said, "I think I'm falling for you." She was feeling the same way, but she just didn't want to face it. They pulled into the parking lot of the hospital. She asked "what are we doing here?" He said "just come on sexy." She climbed out.

Just before they entered, Honcho looked to his left, and sitting there was a van with three men inside. If his gut was right about Tiff and her sisters, they are dead starting with Tiff. Right away he nodded, then went inside. They took the stairs because elevators and Honcho didn't mix. Once they made it to the third level, he walked towards his father's room. They entered and he turned to her and said, I'd like you to meet my dad, Pedro." All the color left her face. She was looking down at the man they were paid to kill. Lee had shot him point-blank in the side of his head. *How could he be alive?* was all she was thinking. She looked at Preston and told him she needed to use the ladies room. Just then, the machine started going crazy. She walked down the hall to the ladies restroom. While she was there trying to figure out what she would do next, she called her sisters to let them know what was going on. What she didn't know was that while she was in the restroom, Pedro came out of his coma.

TO BE CONTINUED . . .

LOADZ 2 Coming Soon

I want to thank my wife, Naketta S. Franks, for believing in me when no one else did. For all of the days I wanted to just give up on life, you gave me the little push that kept me going, and I want you to know that I appreciate you so much, Fat Head. I would like to thank my daughters, Yishenquie and Constance, for the time and effort they put into helping me complete my first novel.

I give a shout out to a young man named Shawn also known as "Broadway" who inspired me to write this book. I never thought I could write a book until I met him in the county jail. Yes, I wrote this in its entirety while I was in the county. Again, I want to say "thank you," Shawn. I never judge a book by the cover. I like to open it up and read it first. You're a good dude at heart, and I pray you succeed in whatever you choose. A big thanks to my baby brother, Dontae. He was there every step of the way. Even when he didn't see my vision he still gave me hella support, and I'm so grateful for that. I've got to thank my little sister, Gregnita. She was hard on me right out of the gate! No matter what I do, she is hard on a brother, but that is what makes her who she is, and I wouldn't trade her for all the money in the world.

This person is special to me for many reasons. I never called anyone Ma since my own mother was murdered, but this woman treated me just as good as she treated her own children. She stole my heart. Merlin Moore was my best friend Anthony Moore's mother (may he rest in peace), but this woman is amazing, caring and loving. I regret that I then got so caught up in life that I haven't been to see her. What kind of son am I? I promise I will do better and I love you.

In loving memory of my biological mother, Constance M. Franks. I would give my life if you could live and meet your grandkids and the women I love with my all. I miss you every day, and I just don't understand why, but I know that you are with me in Spirit. Love you Ma.

In loving memory of these dudes, I am about to name who were my pack when I was young: Leotis Martin, Anthony Moore and William Jackson. I could tell you all kinds of stories from girls to us stealing cars. 103rd and Union were the good ole days. We had fun, and I miss each and every one of yall. Every book I write isn't just for me, it's for all of us. Even when God calls me home, we will live forever through these books. I love and miss y'all!

It's only right I shout out to the individuals that really had real love for me -- my dude Albert aka Pooka, Jamal aka Movie Mall, Mike aka Pink, Loranze aka Fat Boy Lo, Montez aka Tez, Deon aka D, Lamar aka Mut, Anthony aka Ace, Kurt aka Work, Fred AKA Jefe, Andy, Jeff, and a whole bunch more, real recognize real, no frauds allowed.

Free all my niggas! Y'all know who y'all is, and my Little brother Tamar aka Head is on a countdown now. He will be back real soon. All praises to the Almighty!

www.ingramcontent.com/pod-product-compliance
Lightning Source LLC
Chambersburg PA
CBHW031942010726
47493CB00007B/2042